T

THE MEN

Simon Masters was born in 1948 and spent his first eighteen years in Lancashire. His first novel, *Scream a Little Louder*, was published when he was seventeen, and his second, *A Door Closing*, a year later. His third book was a history and documentary account of the National Youth Theatre, of which he was an actor-member between the ages of fifteen and eighteen. Since 1970 he has written for the theatre, films, television and radio, and has script-edited a large number of programmes for the BBC, including *Spy Trap* and *Poldark*. He is married with one son.

TARGET

THE MEN THEY ONCE WERE

Simon Masters

British Broadcasting Corporation

First published 1977 by the
British Broadcasting Corporation
35 Marylebone High Street
London W1M 4AA

ISBN 0 563 17404 8

Printed in England by
Love & Malcomson Ltd
Brighton Road, Redhill, Surrey

The BBC-1 television series *Target* is produced by Philip Hinchcliffe. The main characters are played as follows: Hackett, Patrick Mower; Tate, Philip Madoc; Bonney, Brendan Price; Louise, Vivien Heilbron.

1

Ahead of them, going into the roundabout, the Jaguar waited until the last moment before signalling right. By then they knew they were closing too fast. The voice that crackled with sudden urgency over their radio only confirmed it.

'You're crawling up his arse, Two! . . . He'll clock you!'

But it was too late: they were committed now and swinging after the Jag. For a brief moment, in its driving mirror, they could see Newby's face looking back, then they were able to cut left letting him lose them. The man beside the driver twisted in his seat to keep the Jag in view and watched it complete one full circle of the island, then go into a second. He brought up the mike held tight in his balled fist and spoke fast, flat but urgent.

'He's playing round the mulberry bush . . . Stay back, One!'

There was a brief pause before One came back over the air, sounding almost weary. 'He must've clocked you.'

'I think . . .' the two men exchanged bleak glances '. . . negative. Just being careful is all.'

'You hope,' the driver said softly.

Then, with their speed at a crawl, they waited—wondering whether they'd blown it. Even if Newby was only a third-rate villain, and this only a routine surveillance of the sort they carried out with a regularity that bordered on tedium, still there was that hurt to their professional pride if a pudding like Newby managed to run circles round them. So they waited, feeling slightly sick, as the seconds dragged. Then, through the rough-textured rush of carrier wave, One was calling. 'West! He's heading west! You read me, Three?' And, broken by distance and the bulk of buildings, they heard Three responding, '. . . 'firmative, One . . . Motorway?'

'Looks like.'

The Driver rammed the gear into second, glanced in his mirror, and accelerated into a U-turn; while, drawing further away and fading now, they heard One confirming the Jag's direction. 'He's on the motorway . . . Say again, on the motorway . . . And going!'

Although only mid-afternoon, being a Friday the London exodus had already begun and traffic on the motorway was building. Over to the west the sky lay sullen and heavy, threatening rain, while up on the fly-over, through the gaps between the crumbling Victorian terraces and across the factory roofs, a cross-wind gusted, buffetting the vehicles, tugging at their steering. With the needle of his speedometer hovering around sixty, and trapped in a dense pocket of traffic, Newby sourly resigned himself to a long, hard haul. Each time he emerged from overtaking a lorry the wind slammed him sideways. The steering wheel was juddering in his hands – it always did at this speed; it got better if he went faster but in this traffic and these conditions sixty was tops. Two hours of this, he decided, and he'd be shagged.

Occasionally he glanced in his mirror to see if he could catch a glimpse of the Cortina that had buzzed him on the roundabout. There'd been two men in it, and Newby subscribed to the view that two men travelling alone could only be either queers or cops. But there was no sign of it behind him now and the mild edge of paranoia it had generated was beginning to subside.

His fixation on men travelling together meant he hardly registered the Escort two hundred yards back, driven by a young woman. Her companion was resting his arm against the door with his chin on his hand, the way weary reps ride at the end of a week of motorways. Only hidden in this traveller's hand was a microphone, and over their UHF receiver One was calling, '. . . five miles, then two. Airport turn-off is seven . . . Say again: to Heathrow you have seven miles to run.'

His eyes on the Jag up ahead, the Detective remarked, almost to himself, 'Not going to the bloody airport . . .' and glanced at the girl. 'Is he? Bet you a kiss.'

For a moment she didn't respond, then without looking at him she said, 'Like playing for pennies, is that. Not worth it.'

And he laughed.

As Newby approached the Heathrow turn-off the rain came. It broke without warning, a sudden and violent deluge that transformed the motorway within seconds into a battleground of spray and fumes, and squalling broadsides that thrashed a cross the cars contemptuous of their wipers. Overhead the barrelling thunder of jet-noise from an incoming 747 was all but obliterated by the drumming on the car roofs and the steady slash of wheels churning through water.

Car lights were being switched on as the clouds of spray brought visibility down to a hundred yards or less. Even so, the Escort came on in a sudden surge, ploughing on, almost reckless in the need to relocate the Jag . . . which the girl saw first, grey and blurred, shrouded in the spray of a lorry. She touched her companion's arm and pointed.

He pressed his transmit button and began to call, trying to combat the background din. 'Three . . . D'you read me, One?'

And from a mile further back, 'Three: go.'

'Not the airport – say again: *not* the airport.' Then, releasing the button, he looked to the girl whose face was screwed in a grin of concentration as she tried to gauge the speed and distance of the Jag through the filthy slip-stream of the lorry. Like thinking aloud he said, 'So where?'

But before she could respond, almost as though they'd heard him, One crackled back over the air, 'Stay with him, Three. We'll get Base tell our friends . . . he's on his way.'

Detective Superintendent Steve Hackett was late getting back to the office. He'd been with his boss, Tate, Co-Ordinator Number 13 Regional Crime Squad, talking to the Chief Constables and a man from the National Co-Ordinator's office for most of the day. It had left him feeling drained. Talking money and manpower, logistics and method, and reducing crime – the obscenity of so much crime – into abstract hypotheses was so unlike any operational reality he'd experienced that it built in him a sense of impotence and frustration which, besides wearying, made him irritable and restless. So, while Tate had gone straight home, he'd come back to the office; to find it deserted, and full of the greyness of evening.

Without bothering to switch on any lights he dumped his briefcase on his desk and crossed into the Intelligence Bureau which housed most of the Squad's hardware: the computer terminal, radio transceiver, telex and mufax machines, and the Telstor phone recorder. He tripped the recorder back to zero, waited until the spools had stopped whirring, then switched to play. For a moment there was nothing, then a woman's voice – young, precise, matter-of-fact – began speaking.

'To Detective Superintendent Hackett, from Detective Sergeant Colbert: time . . . eighteen-fifteen hours: begins . . . Further to a call from C-11 at fourteen-o-five hours today, it is confirmed that Peter Robert Newby – say again, Peter Robert Newby – CRO of fifty-four, convictions for theft of motors, assault, unlawful possession of firearms, known associate of a team active in armed robberies in the MPD and in Essex, has left London and is being followed West on the M4 by a surveillance group of C-11 . . .'

Still listening, Hackett meandered towards the windows and stood gazing between the open slats of the venetian blinds out over the lights of the city, winking and pricking through the quickening gloom. It was a sight that never failed to please him: on the one side the great sodium glare of the centre from which one arm swung away to link with another great conflagration at the flyover intersection; on the other, glinting from among distant trees, feeble and sparse, the converted gas lamps on the Heights. Never wholly sure what the term 'beautiful' really meant, this, nevertheless, was a sight he always regarded as beautiful; and it calmed him.

He realised with a jolt that he'd momentarily stopped listening. He turned away from the window and applied his attention once more to the cool, calm voice on the recorder.

'. . . and we are asked to take over the follow on the motorway; the C-11 group will then withdraw. A hitherto . . . er, reliable source for C-11 has said that Newby is coming out to set up a robbery; not known where, or with whom. I am covering C-11 with three teams: me with Dukes; Cubbon with Ikey Baer; and Bonney solo.' There was a brief pause, then, '. . . We'll – er – ring in . . . from wherever we get: message ends.'

He stabbed down the stop button and triggered the recorder back to zero. Then he stood for a moment absorbing what he'd heard. 'One thing for sure,' he thought, smiling slightly, 'if the caper was any bloody good C-11 would've kept this Newby to 'emselves, not punted him out to us peasants.' But be that as it may, somewhere out there, a chase was on; and if he hadn't been sitting getting jaw-ache all day he could have been in on it! Not now, too late now . . . and as another surge of sour anger possessed him he crossed to the radio transceiver and switched on.

Against a background of static and road noise, fading then coming loud again, voices all distorted by the electrics, he could hear them; sometimes flat and laconic, at others terse with an edge of urgency. He settled to listen, feeling almost like a voyeur as the adrenalin began to flow, even though the kicks could only be vicarious.

'See him?'

'No . . . You?'

'Yeah – I see him . . .' this from Ikey Baer, who had fat lips and usually played trumpet in the back rooms of pubs on Friday nights when he wasn't following cowboys like Newby to God-knows-where. 'There's a truck – red truck? He's in behind that truck.'

'Yes! Got him . . .' And that was Louise, Detective Sergeant Louise Colbert, cool and calm Louise. For a moment Hackett found himself pondering the absolute asexuality of her voice. Perhaps it was deliberate, he decided: one of the ploys she'd adopted in order to survive in this company of men, riding the quips and the jokes and the innuendos until now, at least most of the time, they could almost forget she was a woman – even such an attractive one. 'Ikey . . . can you get any closer? Up that hill?'

'Too close up his chuff, he'll clock me.'

'Could lose you – if you don't . . .'

'Hill,' Hackett thought, 'which bloody hill? Where's he taking them? . . .'

'. . . over the hill – could go left,' Louise was saying.

And Ikey retorting, almost tartly, 'Why should he?'

'If he's clocked us . . .'

'Hasn't clocked us!'

'All right! But where's Bonney? . . . Can you raise Bonney?'

Then Ikey was calling, 'Bonney: Ikey . . . Bonney, y'read me? . . .' over and over at intervals until, very faintly, Hackett heard Bonney responding, 'Go, Ikey . . .'

'Where are you?'

And still very faint, 'Airport . . .'

Then Hackett knew which hill they were climbing; and he knew damn sure where Newby was taking them . . .

Dressed all in black leather with a black and red chequered scarf at his throat Bonney sat astride his BMW on the approach road to the airport, scanning the flow of traffic appearing up the hill. At his back, muted and in the distance there was the incoming jet-whine of a One-Eleven, its engine-roar building as it dropped in to land.

But Bonney had eyes only for the road, and for the low, paired headlights of a Jag that should be coming over the brow at any moment. Over the UHF Ikey was calling that they'd lost visual contact, but still he couldn't see the car and beneath his leather he felt sweat suddenly prickling. The road was busier than he'd like – so many lights and the traffic moving in a fast, constant stream – it was too easy to become mesmerised, to make a mistake . . .

He blinked, and, as Ikey called again asking whether he had contact yet, he muttered, 'Shut up, Ikey! . . .' while, behind him, the pitch of the jet-whine was rising to a muted scream as the plane touched down and the pilot threw its engines into reverse.

'Gone by yet?' Ikey was getting louder, must be nearing the top of the hill himself by now . . .

'Negative,' he said tersely.

'Bloody hell! . . .'

Then, emerging from behind a truck which had been obscuring it, slowing and signalling right to turn into the airport, he saw the Jag. Tight into the mike hidden beneath his scarf, and unable to keep the relief out of his voice, he said, 'Airport! . . . And coming in!'

As he heard Ikey responding the Jag rolled smoothly past, close enough for him to catch a brief glimpse of its driver: a small, almost insignificant-looking figure hunched at the wheel, with a pale, sharp-featured face that was soured now in weariness and the boredom of driving.

While he watched the Jag pause at the entrance to the carpark then roll on in, Ikey's Dolomite came off the main road and swept past him. Louise and Dukes shouldn't be far behind. He turned to scan the road again, but before he could actually see them he heard Louise calling, 'That flight that's just in – where from? Anyone know?'

The airport was only a small affair, perched high on a sloping plateau across which, invariably, a cold wind came slicing. For much of each day the place lay dormant bar the occasional, buzzing intrusions of small air-taxis or executive Pipers; but now, along the line of blue lamps marking the taxi-track, with its red anti-collision beacons strobing through the darkness, the One-Eleven was slowly taxiing towards the crouched terminal buildings, the whine of its jets steadily mounting.

Into their scream, splitting the air, Newby stepped out on to the wind-blown terrace. He paused as the cold hit him, dragged his raincoat tight around himself, then crossed to the rail to watch the plane slowly turn in front of the building, and stop. The jet-scream rose in a last, deafening burst before the engines were cut and wailed into silence. Stairs were being nudged against the fuselage and as the aircraft door was opened a customs officer went aboard.

Coming on to the terrace behind Newby Louise saw him in a corner between the wall and rail, huddled against the cold, looking towards the plane. So . . . odds on this was a meet, only with whom? Who, on flight BA 030 in from Paris – which is what the arrivals board downstairs said this was – had Newby come all this way to meet? And why here? Thirty or so flights a day Paris–Heathrow . . . so why here? Casually and unobtrusively she mingled with the other spectators shivering at the rail and watched as the passengers began disembarking.

There were commercial travellers from Rungis, Concorde technocrats home from Sud-Aviation, two nuns, one or two girls, a few late holidaymakers with their bags of duty-free, and an assortment of men who might be anything: cross-Channel commuters, wine merchants, Eurocrats, or even . . . villains flown in for a meet. There was no one there she recognised, no one who stood out, no way, yet, of knowing. In a straggling line with the wind whipping at their hair and clothes they trooped across the concrete beneath the glare of floodlights towards immigration control.

Apparently satisfied, Newby turned from the rail. Almost as though she'd anticipated his move – the way it had to be if she were to remain inconspicuous – Louise turned with him and they joined the eager jostle of people pushing through the door from the terrace.

Down in the terminal concourse Dukes stood at the bookstall absently flicking through a paperback. He'd had a date with his girl that evening, until they'd had the phone call about Newby; she was a waitress and it was her one night off in the week . . . then – bloody Newby! He slapped the book down in disgust and picked up another. After a moment he became aware that the assistant was watching him, looking at him decidedly oddly. It was some time before he realised why: the book he'd picked up was an identical copy to the one he'd thrown down.

He grinned at her. 'This one's better,' he said, honestly.' The girl retreated in confusion.

Out of the corner of his eye he saw people beginning to descend the stairs from the terrace, which was a signal that the passengers should soon be appearing. He edged back into the cover of a swivelling wire book rack and slipped the camera from his raincoat pocket. It was a compact, automatic rangefinder. Used with highspeed film that was then false-processed, it could produce results that were staggering.

Newby and Louise came into sight more or less simultaneously: Newby down the stairs, Louise along the gallery that ran three sides of the concourse. Her sweeping glance found Dukes. With the merest lift of his eyes he told her that he'd seen. Then he waited.

And Newby waited, with his back to a wall and two clear exits in view – the way, for men like him, it had to be.

Out from the immigration hall the first passengers were emerging: a couple of businessmen, two laughing girls, then a family: Mum and Dad, with a young child screaming tears they couldn't quench, too tired at the end of too long a day. The father cuffed the boy's head. embarrassed by the noise and the attention he was creating, almost as though some visible manifestation of his authority was demanded else his manhood would be at stake. The child only cried the louder, and they lurched away towards the doors with their cases and their carrier bags, desperate to be gone.

Behind them, as more passengers spilled out, the small concourse was beginning to take on the atmosphere one expected of airports: a throng of people jostling in cross-currents of movement, little surges and eddies, bursts of animation, pockets of stillness; a couple embracing, parents greeting daughters back from au-pairing, a chauffeur impassively accepting his boss's case. And through it all, softly strolling, and for a long time unmarked, came the Frenchman.

He carried an overnight bag with the logo of Air Algérie on its side. Medium height, powerfully built – though not in any gross way – from his face one might guess he was late forties. It was a hard face, heavily lined, with distinct laugh-lines that seemed incongruous, at odds with the coldness of the eyes – unless one knew they weren't laugh-lines at all, but simply the result of squinting too long in the Algerian sun. It was a face some women would find attractive, if they liked rough trade; and if they weren't frightened by the almost indefinable suggestion of cruelty around the mouth and behind the eyes.

At the seats in the centre of the concourse he paused to glance around, then sat, placing the Air Algérie bag beside him. He was still unmarked.

Dukes's eyes were on Newby, who began to move now, slowly out from the wall on a curving trajectory that would bring him past the seats without it seeming too intentional. Ranging ahead of him Louise's eyes reached the Frenchman. Her pulse-rate quickened slightly. It had to be him. Her look lingered a moment, dwelling on the figure below, then Newby cut across her eyeline, breaking the strange, brief spell.

Beside the seats Newby paused, taking in the Air Algérie bag which was the mark by which he'd been told he would recognise his man. Gazing slowly, impassively around the Frenchman ignored him. Newby fumbled out his cigarettes to cover the moment as he looked about one last time, feeling vulnerable and nervous out there in the open.

Then, without looking at the Frenchman, he said quietly, 'You waitin' for a driver, mate?'

The Frenchman's gaze swung to him and slowly took him in: the small, wiry figure; the sharp, nervous face; the hands cupped around the match lighting a cigarette...

'Je ne vous connais pas,' he said, 'qui êtes-vous?'

Dukes's camera was starting to click now. He didn't even need to put it to his eye. At this distance its wide-angle lens was bound to give them what they needed, so he simply held it at his side and let it click away on automatic.

Newby was shaking his head, not understanding. Almost pained he said, 'I was told you'd speak English.'

Very coldly, enunciating very precisely, the Frenchman said, 'Who are you?'

'Newby.'

There was a brief pause, and Newby felt the other's gaze almost mocking him. Then the Frenchman said softly, but as though he meant it to be remembered, 'Jouffret,' and began to rise.

'Oh yeah . . .' Newby said, not quite able to keep the trace of awe out of his voice, 'yeah . . . I've heard about you.'

2

Hackett parked under the trees about twenty yards from the hotel. From here he could see both the Regency frontage – bathed in floodlights – and the black, almost sheer drop at the back, four hundred feet down to the river. The hotel was one of the landmarks of the Heights. It still had pretentions to exclusivity, yet this was where Newby and the Frenchman had come . . . and the irony of it sourly amused him.

As he climbed from his car and locked the door he heard footsteps approaching. Out of the darkness a figure emerged. It was Bonney, rubbing his hands together as he came, his face a pale blur above the scarf that was pulled almost to his nose.

'Made good time,' Bonney said.

'Still in there?'

Bonney nodded.

'So what're you doing? Wouldn't Louise take you in with her?' Hackett's tone was softly mocking.

'Thought I might look too conspicuous,' Bonney said drily.

'Wouldn't get past the doorman – you. Not dressed like that.'

Bonney sniffed into his scarf. He liked his bike gear – was, as they say, attached to it; only since he'd made sergeant there'd been times when it had seemed as though there was some perverse conspiracy to keep him off bikes altogether. Tonight, riding Newby's tail from the airport had been a joy. He'd even managed to shoot the barriers on the Basin bridge whereas Louise had got herself trapped wrong side of the river.

'Anyway,' he said, 'I'm supposed to hang about 'case they suddenly take off again. Not that they will. Not now.'

'Still, it's all good overtime – innit?' Hackett replied drily.

As he broke away towards the hotel a gust of wind shivered a few leaves down from the trees: already, in the air, there was that soft-sad tang of autumn and the warm light spilling from the windows of the bar ahead seemed already to be offering refuge. 'Going to rain,' Hackett thought absently; then, in one of those odd leaps: 'Skin his arse some day, Bonney will, on that bike; some day, or some autumn night . . . in the rain.'

Through the revolving doors into the foyer he paused to get his bearings. It was some time since he'd been here, but the opulence hadn't changed. It lay beneath one's feet, adorned the panelled walls, hung from the moulded ceilings in cut-glass fountains: it even permeated the air in the soft scent of flowers and aroma of cigar smoke.

The girl at the desk looked up and smiled. He'd have smiled back because she was easy to smile at, but at that moment he saw Cubbon in the resident's lounge, sitting so that he had a clear view of the foyer through to the lifts and stairs. Cubbon had seen him, and over his copy of the evening paper he inclined his head slightly to the right.

Hackett veered away across the foyer, past the entrance to the dining-room, and came casually through the double glass doors into the bar.

It was big enough to be a ballroom. Its high ceiling was intricately patterned in relief moulding. The support pillars had been boxed round with mirror glass so that eye-lines and perspective tended to become confused. Around the edges of the room were alcoved tables with bench seats covered in leather, while the space in the centre was given over to free-standing tables and chairs.

You couldn't say the place was full, but then – it would need a convention of sales reps to achieve that. Nevertheless it was busy enough with sufficient movement and noise for Hackett to be confident no one had clocked him as he entered. He ordered a tonic straight, no ice, which earned him the inevitable, old-fashioned look from the barmaid but by now he'd learned to live with it. Further along the bar Ikey was leaning against the counter, supping a pint, apparently engrossed in a newspaper; he never even looked at Hackett. Across the room Louise and Dukes were sitting at a table hard by one of the pillars. They looked like any young couple, concerned only with each other.

Hackett paid for his drink and began to saunter across. Louise saw him, smiled and gave a small wave, as though to an old friend, inviting him to join them. He drew up a chair and sat.

'Where are they?'

'Behind you,' Louise said, 'over to your left a bit. You can see them in the mirror. Newby's the one with his back to the wall.'

Casually he let his glance drift across the mirror. Newby and the Frenchman were sitting in one of the alcoves close to the fire-exit which gave back on to the street. Newby was pressed tight into the corner from where he could cover the whole bar. The Frenchman had his back to them and looked altogether more relaxed. They were drinking whisky. Newby seemed to be doing most of the talking, the Frenchman just nodding and asking occasional questions.

'Briefing him . . .' Hackett thought, 'or filling him in . . . about something . . .' and wished to God he could see the man's face, because for sure it was the Frenchman who was important.

'They came straight from the airport,' Louise was saying, 'well – more or less . . .'

'Got themselves lost in the Basin,' Dukes explained.

'But that was all it was,' Louise continued. 'They've booked in for two nights . . .' and as Hackett's glance came back to her – the thing he really wanted to know: 'The one who came from Paris . . . is Roland Jouffret.' She pushed a piece of paper across the table for him to read. 'The number's from his passport. I got it from the girl at the desk. And . . .'

'Bruay . . .' Hackett read aloud.

'Yes -- en-Artois. That's where M'sieur Jouffret lives – says he lives.' Then, in response to Hackett's look, 'Gave as his address when he booked in.'

Hackett pocketed the paper. 'All right,' he said quietly, 'so we take it what C-11 told us is right. It's a meet. Only what we still don't know and *need* to know is – why here. Any thoughts, Louise?' She shook her head.

'As a villain,' Hackett went on, 'our Mister Newby looks more like a punter to me. But this other, M'sieur Jouffret . . .'

'He's the hard one,' Louise stated flatly.

'Looks relaxed enough,' Dukes muttered. 'Foreigner? Looks like he owns the place.'

And Hackett said again, 'Why here?'

Briefly they speculated, racking their brains for what it might be that was so important or attractive or enticing as to bring a man like Jouffret from Bruay-en-Artois – wherever that might be – all the way here. They came up with nothing.

The alcove next to Newby and Jouffret was already occupied so there was no way they could get in close enough to listen; besides which, the conversation between the two men seemed to be drying up. They were spending more time with their drinks now, exchanging only the odd word. Jouffret had started to look incuriously around the bar and Hackett was able to catch brief, oblique glances of his face; which was contained and impassive, like the face of a man who's seen enough, done enough, been enough bad places never to be shocked or horrified or moved by anything, ever again.

The detectives felt a sense of deflation beginning to set in. The only thing they could do now was to sit and wait.

This was where the job started to get boring. The hours and hours they'd spent sitting, watching and waiting, time and again, and it was always the same; might, in the end, produce something positive . . . or nothing at all. Only this time, because of the Frenchman perhaps, they each felt a premonition of something.

'Photos?' Hackett said.

Dukes nodded. 'At the airport.'

'And here,' Hackett said, 'if you can.' He collected together their empty glasses and headed towards the bar for another round.

Dukes glanced at Louise who shrugged slightly. He fumbled the camera out of the pocket of his raincoat slung over the back of his chair, and was lost for a moment in the problem of where and how to get the best shot. Suddenly, with a slight start, he felt Louise squeezing his arm hard. She'd stiffened slightly. He risked a quick glance sideways. A man had just arrived at Newby's and Jouffret's alcove and was speaking to them.

He was a big man, bulky and overweight, probably in his middle fifties. Newby was rising now and it looked as though there were introductions going on . . . Jouffret remaining seated throughout, looking coldly and impassively up at the newcomer who eventually eased his bulk down on to one of the benches.

Dukes let his arm hang loose beside his chair. In his hand was the camera. Lost amid the surrounding hubbub it began its rapid click.

In contained excitement Louise's eyes had swung to the bar, searching for Hackett. Her excitement was fast being replaced by shock. Except for Ikey at one end of the counter and a couple at the other there was no one there. Hackett had disappeared.

She found him outside, sitting in the darkness on one of

the benches overlooking the Gorge. A yard or so beyond the bench the ground fell away sheer. The distance across to the woods opposite was maybe quarter of a mile; only now it was all black void into which he sat staring.

She sat beside him and for a moment neither of them spoke. Then she said, 'The third man . . . did you see?'

His face turned towards her, grey and clouded. 'He's why they've come.' He paused. 'I know him. Why I left.'

She waited to see if he'd go on. When he didn't she said, 'Who is he?'

'Bellis. William Archer Bellis.' He paused again. 'Didn't know he was out yet.'

'Someone you put away?'

He nodded. 'Six years ago.'

Again she waited, but when he wasn't forthcoming decided she'd not press him. She'd known Hackett four years now and knew he wasn't often prone to moods like this; but when he was it didn't do to push. Working with this dark-haired, sardonically handsome, ruthless and yet very private man could be volcanic enough without her provoking him. He wasn't easy to work for, or with; insufferable at times; wasn't, she would say, a nice man. But he was good at what he did and although his methods, sometimes, were distasteful she could live with that. And as long as she kept her distance she could respect him enough . . .

She rose and turned, her back to the void and her face catching a faint glow from the lights burning through the rear windows of the hotel.

'So now he's the one we follow?' she asked, only it was more like a statement.

He nodded. 'There'll be a briefing in the office tomorrow. First thing.'

'Night, then.'

He watched her silhouette crossing the line of lighted

windows before being swallowed by the darkness. He sat a moment longer then rose himself, turning up his collar against the wind that ever more strongly promised rain, and began to wander along the path which followed the line of cliff. Ahead, slightly above and seeming to hang in space, were the lights of the bridge across which, at infrequent intervals, car headlights crawled. Over to the right through the wind-tossed trees, feeble street lamps shivered in the darkness. All in all there was little here to intrude on his reverie; and as he strolled with slow, even steps, sifting back through those six-year-old memories, he could almost feel the wind plucking at the mental cobwebs and blowing away the dust that lay there.

Of all of them, the picture that came clearest – and kept coming, ever more vividly – was of Willie Bellis, the way he was when he lurched through the door of that betting office in Picton Street: a stocking over his head, a sawn-off shotgun in his hands, yelling for everyone to hit the floor. The thing that still snatched at Hackett's gut was the memory of that shotgun, pointing right at him, point-blank range, as Willie realised he'd walked into a trap.

Every detective remembers the first time he looks down the wrong end of a twelve bore. Even on subsequent occasions it's never quite the sort of experience one can treat with total equanimity; but that first time! . . .

Willie had uttered a kind of bellow of sick rage. Hackett remembered flinching, anticipating the blast. He'd yelled – something original like, 'Don't be bloody stupid, Willie!' There'd been a blur of red momentarily pulsing across his vision so it was like looking through blood-misted glass . . . but then, almost miraculously, what he'd seen was Willie putting his hands up.

Between walking away and ending up a bloody and

shredded corpse lay what? Only whatever went on in the heads of men like Willie Bellis – flak-happy maniacs – in those split seconds of panic and rage: trapped; caught bang at it; knowing this time they'll go down for five years, or six, or maybe ten or even more . . . bloody coppers! In that instant, some day still to come, one of them would probably pull the trigger. Only that day Willie had put his hands up.

And that was Hackett's first time. The afternoon of the Cheltenham Gold Cup, he remembered. He'd been told later that L'Escargot had won at seven to two, which had seemed almost irrelevant. He'd not had money on anything; not even on staying alive.

Across the tree-patched rise he heard a motorbike firing. It pulled him up as he wondered if it might be Bonney; if Willie was on the move now, going home. Or going someplace with Newby and the Frenchman. He thought of the gross, lumbering figure he'd seen in the bar and he realised now – with some surprise – that that wasn't the Willie of his memories, hard bastard, last of a bad team. The Willie he'd seen back in the bar had looked tired and slow . . . more like an old man. In a strange way it almost depressed him. Not that he was sorry for Willie, it wasn't quite that; only that somehow it was sad to see a figure who'd been a potent force once lumbering and wheezing and over the hill now, like some punch-drunk, broken boxer.

It made Hackett wonder if his eyes had deceived him: because if that was what the last six years had turned Willie into – what was he doing here now with Newby and this Hardman from France? Not in their league, especially not Jouffret's if Hackett was any judge, not now. It didn't make sense. What could Willie Bellis possibly have that was of interest to them?

It made him ponder the whole business afresh, and

again he came up against the same question: why here? Six years ago he'd have known where, maybe, to look for an answer because six years ago Willie had had connections. There wasn't a job Willie pulled that hadn't been planned by the man who ran him – who ran that whole team of armed robbers, of whom Willie had been the last to go. It occurred, sourly, to Hackett that if Willie had known then who'd betrayed him – set him up to be lifted – and why . . . who could say what might have happened? Poor bastard. He wondered if Willie ever knew – even now – who'd put the bubble in for him to be lifted. In a surge of disgust that was like bile in his mouth he tasted the memory of an old obsession.

Willie may have been a hard bastard, but not evil. Not in the way some others were evil, like the one who'd fingered him – whom Hackett had never caught. The bitterness of that still lay hard and uncompromising within him.

Borne on the wind came the first drops of rain, heavy like spent shot, grazing his cheek. Bleakly he turned, hunching into his collar, and started across the grass back towards his car.

Tate was a small, stocky Welshman, shrewd and tough, with a voice that could have halted the traffic in the city centre if he'd really decided to use it. Most times a veneer of soft Welsh courtesy lay deceptively upon him, but that hid the flint and steel of his true nature. Tate was an experienced, pro copper. In a way he'd made a mistake getting himself promoted to Detective Chief Super because that had put him behind a desk, keeping him off the streets which was where he felt he truly belonged. Perhaps that's why he drove his Squad so hard, riding Hackett's back like a hunter to hounds: sparing in praise or encouragement, abundant in his condemnation if the horse should stumble, and suffering fools not at all.

In return he protected his men with a jealous zeal against all attack, be it from Chief Constable or disgruntled Force CID officer – and more than once Steve Hackett had been thankful for that. He had the craftiness of a Welsh horsedealer, the tenacity of a hill farmer, and just occasionally the turn of phrase of a Bard. Among the members of his Squad he enjoyed a loyalty that was enviable.

On Saturdays he usually came in just to open the mail and read the Daily Report, but this morning he'd found himself in the middle of an informal briefing which, on his appearance, had decamped itself into his office that was full now with Hackett and himself, Louise, Bonney, Dukes and Baer.

For Tate's benefit Hackett had retracked and was now filling them in on William Archer Bellis. 'Last of a bad team,' he was saying. 'Tried to knock over a betting shop in Picton Street. Afternoon of the Cheltenham Gold Cup. L'Escargot won . . .' which raised one or two quiet laughs. 'Willie got nine years in an indictment for armed robbery – three counts. I was officer in the case.'

'Got his D/F?' This from Tate.

Louise handed across a copy of Bellis's CRO form which Tate quickly scanned.

'You were . . . ?'

'Detective Chief Inspector, sir.'

'And you arrested him?'

'Yes, sir.'

'How?'

There was a flicker of hesitation on Hackett's part before he said, 'Informant.'

Tate gave him a long, baleful stare that was like saying, 'Not bloody good enough: just – "informant" . . .' So Hackett shrugged and told them. What the hell? There was no one he had to protect now; hadn't been even then. He'd been used.

'It was his wife,' he said. 'She was having it away – with the fella who set Bellis up. Name of Harry Smith. Bellis used to run for him, along with a team of others: only we knocked them over, one by one. And Willie was the last. They stitched him for us – Smith and Willie's wife . . .' bleak disgust fraying the edge of his voice slightly.'. . . So they could go off and live high on what he'd made them. While he went down for nine.' He paused briefly. 'I didn't know that at the time, of course. Never did get Smith. He just . . . dropped out of sight.'

There was a short silence, then Tate nodded gently. 'So when did he get out, this Bellis?'

'Week ago Wednesday, sir,' Louise told him. 'But before that he'd been working out, on the Prison Hostel Scheme. On the docks.'

Tate nodded again. 'So,' he said, gently drawing it all together, 'we've got Newby, who C-11 say is a robber, comes all the way down from London to meet with Bellis, who *was* a robber – around the time L'Escargot won the Cheltenham Gold Cup, and Mister Hackett lifted him; which was years ago, so he's got to be over the hill now . . . Plus the one from France.'

'Jouffret,' Louise offered.

'What do we know about him? Jouffret?'

Hackett and Louise exchanged edgy glances.

'You'll have got off a signal to Interpol,' Tate said.

'Not yet.' Hackett sounded almost defensive. 'Take for ever if we go through Interpol. Bloody third-rate Post Office is Interpol. I'll talk to the French direct.'

'Rather you than me,' Tate said drily. 'All right: now tell me what happened last night, from where Mister Hackett clocked him.'

It didn't take long. Virtually nothing had happened.

Newby, Jouffret and Bellis had talked until just after midnight. It had seemed to Louise that Bellis and Jouffret weren't getting on too well, but she could have been mistaken. Then, around twelve-fifteen, Newby and Jouffret had gone up to their rooms, presumably to sleep; while Bonney had followed Willie home – to a crumbling rooming house in Baltic Street, which was one of a maze of dirty, ragged streets in the Old City. The house had looked as though it should have been condemned years ago.

Loose surveillance had been maintained during the night but nothing and no one had stirred. But this morning, around O-nine-hundred-hours, Newby and Jouffret had left the hotel. They'd taken the Jag, picked up Bellis from Baltic Street, and now they were being followed again.

It wasn't much; indications, only, that something was possibly in the making. All very well to say that with a trio like Newby, Jouffret and Bellis, criminal intent could be assumed a certainty. But what criminal intent? Without knowing that, proof of association was worthless: which is just what Tate was saying – that in his opinion what Hackett had got so far was precisely bugger all – when there was a knock at the door and Tom Cubbon stuck his head in. Cubbon had been manning the radio transceiver ever since the follow had been resumed that morning. His glance sought out Hackett.

''Scuse me, sir . . . but they've stopped. We've got them located.'

'Where?'

'Looks like it's the docks. Spent a bit of time sniffing round Jamaica Street, then they drove on in. Now they're on foot. Inside.'

Hackett felt a small surge of excitement. 'Thanks, Tom.' Suddenly something was making sense – something that had been troubling him ever since he'd seen Bellis the night before. Like pieces of a jigsaw falling into place, the watching and the waiting were beginning to make a pattern out of chaos. In his mind the operation had just slipped gently into gear: because if Willie Bellis had been out on the prison hostel scheme, working on the docks . . . where else would they be? Willie *knew* the docks: and *that* was what made him useful to Newby and the Frenchman . . . had to be! It seemed so obvious now, so logical.

As soon as the others had got his drift the meeting began to break up. Even Tate was now agreeing that it looked as though they had an operation. Ikey and Dukes left to join the surveillance in the docks while Louise was to begin trying to contact the Police Judiciaire – in Bruay or Arras, or Béthune or Lille – to make enquiries about Jouffret. Bonney had the worst job: he was to be long-stop in Baltic Street. If the surveillance teams lost their mark, sooner or later Willie Bellis would be bound to go home.

As Hackett made to follow the others Tate called him back. 'This Willie Bellis,' he said casually. 'Last of a bad team, you said. Only he wasn't, was he?'

Hackett wasn't with him.

'There's the one you didn't get.'

'Harry? Harry Smith?'

Tate nodded gently. 'Bother you?'

'Yes.'

'Even after so long?'

'Always will.'

Tate nodded and paused a moment, wondering how to say what had to be said; not that he cared about Hackett's sensibilities, but sometimes things were more effective if insinuated rather than spelt out. 'Yes . . . Occurred to me while you were talking about Bellis, you sounded almost . . . might say – sorry for him.'

Hackett knew where his boss was driving. 'Not that sorry.'

' 'Cos if he's in on some caper . . .' Tate continued, then tailed off, vaguely.

'Hope he is,' Hackett replied, with a hard, bleak smile. 'Easy to keep tabs on is our Willie. Not so fast on his pins as he used to be.'

'Heartless bastard, aren't you, Steve?' Tate said calmly.

'Thought that was the way you liked it . . . Sir,' Hackett replied evenly.

Bonney sat at the wheel of the Capri gazing along the terraced row of dilapidated tenements. Baltic Street stank ever so vaguely of bad drains and fish and chips. Rubbish stirred in the gutters. The pavements were uneven, weeds poking up between the cracked slabs, while the houses themselves gave off the faint odour of decay. There'd been no fresh paint down Baltic Street in years. Grimy drapes hung at dirty windows, and here and there was an odd house empty, brutally boarded against squatters.

Playing across the pavement about half way down the street were three very young children in cut-down, second-hand clothes that were grey with grime. The two elder girls were bullying their bare-arsed brother, pushing and pulling him in and out of the gutter, enthusiastically slapping his face and hands whenever he tried to stuff grit or insects into his mouth. Their persecution of him was accompanied by squeals of glee.

For a while Bonney had found them a diversion. Now he was bored. The house Willie Bellis lived in was on the other side of the street a bit further down. Its paintwork was faded and peeling. The iron railings around the basement steps were eaten with rust. Hard against them stood an overflowing dustbin and about a dozen empty, unwashed milk bottles. No one had been in; no one had come out. The limp, grey net curtains hadn't moved. Bonney's radio had been silent for the past hour and he was starting to become restive. Surveillance of a moving target could be boring enough, but this . . .

As he crossed towards the house he still had no clear idea of what it was he was intending: simply, it seemed better to be out of the car, and moving. Across the street the children watched him with bold, challenging eyes. He felt somehow naked and exposed, faintly ridiculous to their gaze.

Ambling past the house he cast an incurious glance over its façade. Behind the net at several of the windows curtains were still undrawn. In the basement area were one or two old mattresses reared against the wall, rusty springs poking through the fabric; and an ankle-deep waste of empty bottles and litter. The basement was unoccupied, with chicken wire nailed across the windows, most of which, nevertheless, were smashed.

Once past he paused, wondering what the hell he should do now. The kids were still watching him, unsettling in their steadfast, almost hostile scrutiny. He began to wish he'd stayed in the car. This was a futile exercise anyway. He could only walk past once more, and what could the front of a house tell him? What *would* be good would be to get inside . . . and even as the thought occurred there came another: if this was what they thought, a seedy rooming house, chances were the door wouldn't be locked.

The kids were moving now, slanting across the street towards him in a casual, aimless drift that was somehow almost menacing. He felt threatened – ludicrously. Any moment one of them was going to accost him, ask him what he was doing or what he wanted; and kids were hard to deceive, tyrannical in their persistence. He started back, then turned in suddenly and went fast up the steps to the front door. Behind him one of the girls called, 'Mister . . . You – Mister!' he turned the handle and pushed; and with a wave of relief he felt the door give.

The hall was gloomy, decrepit, and smelt of cats, stale milk and stale, sweaty lives. The walls had once been yellow but were now patchy brown with chipped, bilious orange woodwork. On the floor lay cracked, black and yellow check linoleum. The stale, smothering stench made him retch slightly. From upstairs somewhere he could hear a gramophone playing something loud and brash. Otherwise the place was quiet with the sort of quietness that suggests furtive, creeping lives behind closed doors. Treading softly he started up the creaking stairs.

His exact intention was still hazy in his mind, except that now he was in the building it began to seem only logical for him to get inside Willie's room. Otherwise what was he doing here? This stinking, public part of the house told him as little as its façade, except that for those who lived here it had to be a last resort. Better even this than the bomb-site or the public bench. The vulgar music, muffled behind a closed door, swelled as he climbed, but at least it obscured the creaking of the stairs.

Faintly nagging at the back of his mind Bonney knew what he was likely about to do was illegal. All well and good to scuff out Willie's drum armed with a warrant; but he wasn't, had never really thought or intended to be here. Somehow, he felt, it had just . . . happened. For a moment he debated whether he shouldn't go back, now: before he ran the risk of compromising himself completely. But now he was here, where was the harm? A quick butchers and he'd be away again; and no one would know he'd ever been. Besides – what if he found something significant? Hackett had once said of him – and Bonney had never been sure how far he'd been joking – that he couldn't detect his way out of a paper bag. It nagged at him still, even though he'd made sergeant now; still he was determined one day to prove Hackett devastatingly wrong. And it might just be today.

The first landing offered him a choice of three doors. From behind one of them came the music. He bent to read the scrawled name on a card pinned to the next. As he did so he was vaguely aware of the music coming suddenly clearer. He caught a movement out of the corner of his eye and straightened abruptly.

The woman was in her forties. She was wearing blue, fluffy mules and a flesh-pink satin negligée. In her arms she cradled a large, yellow-eyed, ginger cat. Her bleach-blonde hair was heavily bouffed, but the face was still naked revealing lines and blemishes and pouches of sagging skin that were rapidly turning her into an old crone.

She said, 'Wod you want, my love?'

Her voice was an acid whine. Bonney struggled to respond, realised he was edging backwards, and floundered. She was leering at him: leaning there in her doorway, the music swelling past her, her thick fingers softly stroking the cat . . . and it came to him in a sudden spurt of revulsion – she was *fancying* him!

He said vaguely, 'Er – sorry . . .' somehow forcing a smile back at her. 'Er – rooms? . . . A room?' It was the best he could think of.

Her smile became a touch less predatory. A room meant he was stopping so she could afford to take her time. 'You should've rung, my love,' she said, and he wasn't sure whether the tone was meant to be seductive or reproachful: probably both. 'Still, never mind – eh! I like getting took by surprise . . .'

'Yeah, I'm sorry . . .' he said awkwardly.

'You mind sharin'?'

'Sharing? . . . Oh! – Er . . . No, I wouldn't want to – er . . .'

'Come from the Reverend, have you?'

The question threw him afresh, but luckily she didn't wait for his response. ' 'Cos I did tell him – who he sent'd have to share with the other.' She was bending to put down the cat. When she straightened she'd somehow contrived to ease the negligée down over her shoulder slightly. She said, like making a joke of it, 'Share *me*, lover, if you like . . .' only he knew she meant it.

'Other?' he said, like grabbing at a straw.

'Other he sent.'

'Oh yeah! That'd be . . .'

'Mister Bellis,' she nodded. 'Was you on the Hostel with Mister Bellis?'

Dimly Bonney began to perceive that if only he could survive the next few minutes the plan that'd brought him here – if it could be called a plan – was still possible: more than that – the woman was actually going to help him.

'Yeah,' he lied, 'I – er . . .' and tailed off, because lies were tricky little things that could trap you.

She took his hesitation to be reticence for a different reason. Her smile became all sympathy and understanding. She didn't want to scare him off now.

'Lissen, lover: I don't want to know what form you got if you don't want to tell me. I understand . . .' She laughed, but somewhere in her throat the laugh turned into a cough that took some time to stifle. Recovering, she patted her breast in a way that was incongruous in its delicacy. She was already smiling at him again, as though there'd been no interruption. 'You know what they used to say? Got to qualify for Preventive Detention – before you can get in at Marcia's. See?' She risked another small laugh, and this time she got away with it.

Bonney was nodding dumbly.

'That's who I am, see? – Marcia . . .' She waited for him to respond. He didn't. He just shuffled nervously and forced another aimless grin. She decided to change tack. 'Per'aps you're wantin' to look at the room – eh?'

Before Bonney could reply there was the sound of the doorbell ringing downstairs, long and raucous. Marcia swore under her breath. She took a room key from a table just inside her door and handed it to him.

'Number Three,' she said, nodding across the landing, 'on'y keep your head down: 'cos that could be the cow from Social Security, and what she don't know don't cut the bleedin' benefits. Do it, my love – eh?'

With a sense of relief that was almost euphoric Bonney watched her start away down the stairs. But he didn't have time to linger. He moved, fast; unlocked the door of number three and stepped inside.

Instantly the stale air, full of body odour and dead smoke, turned his stomach over. He swallowed hard, and slowly, bleakly, looked around the room.

It was a poor place to call home. Everything – from the cracked, worn linoleum to the plastic, fly-spotted lampshade – was old, ugly and unutterably depressing. There were two beds, one slept in and unmade, the other bare to its stained, flock mattress. At the side of the first was a wash stand with dirty shaving gear lying on it. In the bowl there was still water, grey and fetid with the scum of shaving soap and bristle. Beneath the bed, just visible behind the sagging chaos of blankets, Bonney could see an old, shabby suitcase. Jammed between the grimy windows stood a dressing table, its top littered with grubby underwear, a newspaper, a belt, and an ashtray overbrimming with the pinched, stained butt-ends of roll-ups.

In the far corner was a wardrobe with its door hanging open. Except for a few bent wire hangers on the rail it was empty.

And that was it. No chair, no carpet, no scrap of comfort against the chilling despair of the place: somewhere not fit for even a lonely loser like Willie Bellis to shuffle out his days in. Difficult to believe Hackett, Bonney thought, looking at this: that once Willie had been a man to reckon with; hard man, living on crime and living well.

The suitcase was locked. To get into it he'd have to force it and although it was odds-on Willie would think Marcia had been snooping he couldn't afford to take too many risks. Irritated he shoved it back under the bed. The drawers of the dressing-table were almost equally frustrating, revealing nothing except a shirt or two, socks, clean pants – the usual and not much of it.

He straightened and looked around again: nothing! All the worldly goods still left to William Archer Bellis were here; pathetic scraps. Only instead of making Bonney feel sad he felt cheated and was beginning to hate Willie. He'd not run so many gauntlets for this. His depressed glance drifted across the top of the dressing-table: not even a letter; not even a scrap of paper – nothing!

But then – very vaguely – something about the open newspaper struck him as odd: the print was too tight in columns that were too narrow. Carefully he lifted aside a dirty vest and saw that it wasn't an ordinary newspaper: it was a copy of *Lloyd's List*, two days old, open at the pages showing the worldwide movement of shipping. Three entries had been ringed in biro.

In accelerating excitement he remembered where Willie had been working while on the Hostel scheme; the same place he was now, with Newby and the Frenchman . . . *in the docks!* Those three ringed entries jumped off the page at him: whatever it was Willie and the others were planning, it had to do with one of those ships. And he loved Willie now, loved him! – poor, careless bastard that he was.

He started to scribble the names of the vessels onto the back of his cheque book: *Swan Royal*, *Swan Hunter*, *Swan Castle* . . . and the fact they were all called Swan something had to be significant too, somehow.

His excitement and concentration was such it wasn't until he heard the door close he realised he was no longer alone. He swung, startled, expecting to see Marcia. Instead there was a man standing there. Bonney had time only to take in the awesome height and girth of the figure, the hook-nosed face with eyes that were trained on him like shotgun muzzles, before the man started to move, closing on him. Hard against the dressing-table Bonney instinctively braced himself for the attack. But it never came.

The man stopped short, towering over him. 'And who the hell are you,' he said, in a voice that was savage and unmistakably Welsh, 'who says he's been sent by me!?'

3

Louise was finding the phone call hard going. It wasn't anything to do with the language – her French was next to perfect – but by ignoring official channels like Interpol one laid oneself open to all manner of complications.

In the first place it had taken her twenty minutes even to get through to the Police Judiciaire in Béthune, whose area of responsibility included Bruay. But that had been merely the beginning of the saga. The real killer had proved to be le Weekend. She'd always regarded it an essentially British institution – or disease, depending on the way you looked at it – but today she'd begun to wonder whether the Police Judiciaire hadn't shut up shop altogether for the whole two days. She'd been shunted from one dead extension to another; left hanging on for interminable periods, unsure even whether she'd been cut off or simply abandoned and forgotten. In the end she'd felt like some lost soul condemned to wander the telephone wires eternally in search of someone to talk to.

Eventually she had managed to raise some young agent de police, however, who'd been altogether thrown by a call from England, unsure of the protocol, and guarded therefore: especially when she'd explained the nature of the information she was seeking. His immediate response had been – why not go through Interpol? Suffering from a mild sensation of déjà-vu, she'd talked as persuasively as she knew how, of the delays involved and the urgency of their need-to-know, but he'd obviously remained unconvinced. He'd taken her number and said he'd ring back.

That was fair enough if he was wanting to check her bona fides, but what wasn't quite so palatable was his keeping her waiting for nearly two hours. He must have been trying to get clearance from above, she'd decided, and obviously hadn't got it because when the return call came he still wasn't sounding too happy. If she could wait until Monday, he'd suggested, she could talk to Commissaire Vatan who'd probably be only too pleased to help, but as things were today . . .

She knew damn sure Hackett wouldn't wear that, so now she was having to grit her teeth, be nice to the guy, and try to coax the information out. It wasn't easy.

'. . . Oui – cet homme qui s'appelle Bellis, il est ancien

voleur . . . Oui . . . Alors: cet homme Roland Jouffret . . . qui habite Bruay-en-Artois, oui . . . Ah! – er . . .' She pulled the operations log towards her to refresh her memory. 'Trente-six, rue Gambetta . . . et en écrivant à l'hôtel sa fiche, il dit que le numéro de son passport est quatre-zéro-sept-neuf, zéro-six . . .'

She heard the young man repeating the number, but what he went on to say she missed entirely, because at that moment the office door opened and a PC from downstairs ushered in a figure, the sight of whom momentarily transfixed her.

He was tall and powerful of build, wearing a black coat that flapped at his calves as he moved. Given his size and black bulk, his rugby-bashed face with its hook nose and imperious eyes that had fixed on her, he was one of the most formidable men she'd seen – and that included any of the villains she'd known. So it intrigued her all the more to see the flash of white at his throat. It wasn't a normal clerical collar; only a thin, white band around the neck-rim of his black, polo-necked sweater.

Into the phone she said quickly, 'Pardon, M'sieur – ne quittez pas!' and put it down on the desk, returning her attention to this bruiser of a parson.

'Shouldn't have broken off just for me,' he said. The voice was Welsh. 'Detective Superintendent Hackett, where would I find him?'

'Is he expecting you?'

'Oh yes! Indeed!'

Louise smiled slightly. There was something about his tone, emphasised by the Welsh lilt, that told her trouble had come for Steve Hackett. She nodded and pointed across to Hackett's door. The man of God started to turn abruptly, paused, nodded 'Thank you', then strode away across the office, the black raincoat flapping in the violent wake of his step.

Louise picked up her phone again, but didn't speak until she'd seen him knock, open the door and enter. As the door closed behind him she said, 'Allô, M'sieur? Pardon; Je suis navrée . . .' while at the same time she was thinking, 'Look out for your soul, Steve . . . if you have one.'

'Griffiths,' the Reverend said, hard as rock. 'Dewi Griffiths.'

'Hackett,' replied the other in kind, 'Detective Superintendent.'

Griffiths held the policeman in the vice of his eyes and paused a long moment while he turned the screw. At the end of it he knew what he was against; Hackett's gaze hadn't faltered. 'Know who I am?' he said at last.

'Now I see you . . .'

'Sin bosun; Maker's Rep . . . Chaplain to the prison where Mister Bellis did his bird!'

And that did throw Hackett slightly. But he recovered fast so there was hardly a pause. 'Really? Well, of course, I have heard . . .'

'What?!'

'Of the work you do: the *good* work you do.' The emphasis on 'good' might almost have been taken as a sneer.

'Soft touch with the slags,' Griffiths sneered back, '*that* what you heard?'

Hackett stood his ground calmly. 'What I heard, you'd have been capped for Wales . . . if you'd not been such a wicked bastard down the blind side.'

Griffiths roared with laughter, showing off the gaps in his teeth. 'An' *that*, good boy, while I was in The-o-logical College, even!'

Hackett smiled thinly, waiting for him to finish laughing. He knew it would be dangerously easy to like Griffiths, to become beguiled by him; and because he had a sure suspicion of what was coming he knew he must keep a distance between them.

'Anyway, Reverend: what is it you want?'

'To know, sir, what *you* want – with Bellis.'

'My business.'

'And his.'

'But not yours,' Hackett said evenly. 'Least not if I can help it.'

His words confirmed Griffiths' fears: there was to be a fight; Hackett had no charity; and Willie Bellis had become a battleground. His face filled, suddenly, with bleak anger, as the devil he lived with stirred. Still managing to keep his voice low, he said, 'You sent a man to search his room.'

'Not sent,' Hackett replied, 'not to search. If that's what he did...'

'He had no right!' Griffiths' voice was beginning to rise now.

'If that's what he did! ...' Hackett repeated.

'Do you doubt my word? And do you tell me, *sir* – you did not know?' Hackett started to shake his head, but Griffiths rode contemptuously on. 'There are no bad soldiers; only bad officers!'

For the first time Hackett felt stung. In cold anger he said, 'If you want to make a formal complaint in accordance with section 49 of the Police Act...'

Again Griffiths overrode him. 'What I want, *sir* – all I want – is that you leave a poor wretch be!'

'Leave him to you?' Hackett charged back, his own voice rising. 'For the sake of his immortal bloody soul?'

'Don't you believe... in an immortal soul?'

'What I believe,' Hackett said, hot into battle now, 'is that William Archer Bellis is conspiring with others to commit... some crime!'

'Then tell him so! Tell him you know what he is at: and stop him!'

'No! If I tell him – or you do – my operation's blown!'

'That all that matters to you, Mister Hackett – is it?'

And Hackett knew damn sure by his own lights – yes, it bloody was! Only this God-botherer was confusing the issues, so nothing was as clear-cut as it ought to be – had to be. He struggled to find the pure simplicity of his argument, the thing he lived by, the end that justified the means he used and the people he broke on the way.

'If this operation gets blown, the ones he's with, next week or next month . . . or next *year* . . . will hit some place where I – or the likes of me – won't be; and maybe they'll blind some bank clerk with ammonia, or blast some poor bastard's head off! So – I'll let them run; and when they hit us . . . I'll be there and I'll take them. All of them! And that's why neither I – nor you! – will drop any easy word to Willie. Right, Reverend?'

Griffiths looked at him for a long moment, pain showing in his eyes, along with disgust and anger that God's world required men to make this sort of choice over other men: and that his dog-eared faith must be tested and torn yet again.

When, at length, he spoke, his voice was weary with contained despair. 'Poor bloody infantry in your fight against crime. That's all Willie is to you. Only I know – I was there and saw it – the lot of poor bloody infantry in a war – is death.'

Hackett shrugged. 'Shouldn't have joined the infantry. Should he?'

There was a pause, and neither of them moved. With a sad trace of his former sparring self, Griffiths said. 'Don't you forget there's infantry on your side too. Why did *you* join, Mister Hackett?'

He didn't expect an answer. He was moving for the door . . . and was gone.

Hackett sank slowly into his chair. He felt suddenly mentally drained now, and still vaguely confused: as though someone strange had been into the familiar room of his life and had rearranged all the furniture; so now he must either learn the new layout or remember where each piece had been and put it back. He was also aware of a slowly rising level of anger although at first its cause evaded him: then he remembered . . . that stupid young bastard Bonney!

There was a knock at his door. He saw Louise through the glass and waved her in. He knew she must have heard something of what had passed between him and the parson, but there was no sign of it. She was as cool and calm and matter-of-fact as always, remote in that self-contained way of hers. He admired her self-control; except when the devil was on him and then it aroused in him a malicious urge to tear down the shutters and see her naked in the window. The only thing that stopped him – the best defence she had although she didn't know it – was simply she was too good an officer for him to risk losing her.

'Jouffret,' she said, 'they know him in Bruay. Where he lives – in the rue Gambetta – it's a pension, the Hôtel Boule d'Or. He came there from Calvi, Corsica. And he's strongly suspected, they say, of – braquages? . . .' She hesitated, unsure of the strict translation. 'Armed robbery? . . . At Gap . . . and at Clermont-Ferrand.'

'And here,' Hackett said softly. 'Sure as hell . . . Right here.'

It wasn't altogether unexpected intelligence. They'd each known what Jouffret was – what he had to be – almost from the first moment they'd seen him. But the confirmation of it brought a chilling sense of reality, all the same. Strongly suspected of braquages, of armed robbery; and they were each thinking of the Frenchman's face. Louise had seen his eyes and had never been in any serious doubt that there was evil there.

Hackett felt a small flip of anticipation and his adrenalin flow that shade faster. It was all building: the pieces of the jigsaw, the tempo of their operation. They knew who, and they knew where: Newby, Jouffret and Bellis; in the docks. All that was left now . . . was what? And when? Everything was going exactly right. Until he remembered again: that bloody young idiot Bonney.

'That God-botherer . . .' he said, feeling his anger rising once more, 'he caught Bonney scuffing out Bellis's room.'

Louise's face jerked to him, startled and alarmed.

'Turning it over. Caught him doing it.'

She said, 'We're blown then,' softly appalled.

Hackett shook his head slowly. 'No, I think not. But we could have been.'

He rose suddenly and went storming past her, letting the anger all come now and have its way.

'Tom!' He yelled from the doorway. 'Where's Bonney?'

From inside the Intelligence Bureau Cubbon called back, 'Not sure. Want me to raise him?'

'Just get him back here!' Hackett yelled. 'Now!'

Newby, Jouffret and Bellis turned the corner into Jamaica Street. It was the second time they'd been here, but now they were on foot, Newby and Jouffret flanking Bellis, Jouffret with his arm around him.

Jamaica Street was a short, dusty approach to one of the main dock gates. Along one kerbside were a few poor trees, irregularly planted, that never seemed quite green. The pavement opposite was raised above the road with ornate Victorian railings along its edge. Hard against the dock gates stood a club for Merchant Seamen, and next to that a dingy, sad hotel for sailing-day wives. Then there were the shipping agents and marine solicitors and import-export offices one after another down the length of the street.

From the doorway of the Famagusta Club Dukes watched the three men come, past the ship's chandlers and the marine bookshop, talking as they strolled, looking for all the world like seamen off any grotty old banana boat. Oh – but what wouldn't he have given, Dukes thought, to hear what they were saying. His eyes scanned the street. With the dock gates at one end and a level crossing at the other one thing was sure: they weren't planning a hit here in Jamaica Street itself – not unless they were mental. It was a boxed-in trap of a place. So what was here that was of enough interest to bring them back a second time?

Eyes back to the three men, he was in time to see Bellis suddenly shaking himself free of Jouffret's arm, and it was done in more than just petty irritation. A brief confrontation followed that had a distinctly ugly quality to it, Bellis snarling something at Jouffret, and the other laughing, right back into his face, taunting him. Then Newby edged between them and gradually managed to get them apart. Sullenly Bellis turned away, leaning against the rail to stare across the street with his back to the others. Behind him Newby was talking urgently to Jouffret while the latter continued to grin. Like a bleeding maniac, Dukes thought.

He made a mental note to remember to tell Hackett that Jouffret and Bellis weren't exactly on the best of terms. Then he recalled that was something Louise had mentioned after they'd first seen them together in the bar. Well – she'd been right; and by the looks of it the relationship had soured even further.

Newby had come to the rail to join Bellis and was talking to him with low urgency, obviously trying to mend the breach, and finally it looked as though the cracks had been papered over because they all began to move off, Bellis a little way in front. They were coming further down the street towards the dock gates, and were going to pass Dukes on the other side of the road at any moment. His camera was in his pocket; and in the dusty shadow of the doorway he decided he could risk just one shot. And then they did something that couldn't have been more helpful if they'd tried: they stopped; not opposite him but just oblique enough for him still to have cover, yet be able to see their faces.

They were standing at the rail outside the office of a shipping line. Bellis was doing the talking, the other two just listening. Occasionally one of them might glance to the office or to the kerb below where cars were parked, but they were glances devoid of any obvious significance, idle and incurious.

Dukes had them in his viewfinder now, and at the top of the frame he saw his shot included the name of the shipping line, gold letters on a blue ground: Gulf America. It made a nice composition, he thought; and triggered the shutter on his camera.

Standing almost to attention in Hackett's office Bonney was facing his boss. He was being roasted. Hackett had left him in no doubt of that. His eloquence had reached heights of ferocity that Bonney seriously doubted had ever been scaled before.

The overall drift of Hackett's tirade could be summed up quite easily: Bonney was a walking disaster area, a liability, not fit to be a copper. Because no good copper – not even any half-good copper! – would act as he had.

Without authority, wholly illegally, he'd put himself out on a limb and it had snapped right under him. He'd come within an ace of blowing the operation, and even closer than that to publicly discrediting the Squad. And if either of those things *had* happened . . . !

If Bonney hadn't been aware of the odd occasions Hackett himself had bent the rules – if ever so slightly – to suit the exigency of the moment, he'd have felt more uncomfortable than, in fact, he did. As it was he half suspected Hackett of saying what had to be said for the sake of form; not that he didn't believe Hackett meant all of it, but not, perhaps, in so rigid a fashion as his tone implied. After all, weren't there areas, unacknowledged grey areas, where the maxim of 'do what I say but not what I do' had to apply? This was one of those grey areas. The code of police conduct had been laid down to protect the greater good – the rights of the innocent. But Bonney had also acted, in his eyes, for the greater good: Willie Bellis, Peter Robert Newby and Roland Jouffret had to be stitched. End of case.

Hackett's tirade seemed to be drawing towards a close now. Some of the fire had gone out of it. He was saying, '. . . and you get caught ever again, Sergeant, scuffing through some villain's room without benefit of . . .'

'Clergy, sir?' Bonney said helpfully.

'A warrant to search, Sergeant! . . . I'll have those stripes off you and boot you back to Traffic Division! You read me?'

'Yes, sir. If I get caught ever again.'

Hackett thought he detected a slight emphasis on the word 'caught'. Bonney's face remained impassive. Very coldly and deliberately Hackett said, 'I couldn't afford you. Couldn't afford to keep you. Savez?'

There was a brief pause, then Bonney nodded.

'All right,' Hackett said wearily, letting the last of his

anger drain out of his voice. 'So?'

'Sir?'

With a kind of weary patience Hackett said, 'What was *there*?'

'Oh!' And Bonney grinned. From his inside pocket he took a fold of paper and spread it on the desk for Hackett to read. 'Only odd thing was a copy of *Lloyd's List* – gives details of movement of shipping, all that, you know?'

Hackett nodded: he knew.

Bonney indicated the paper. 'These are the names of three ships, all sailing to the UK.' He paused fractionally for effect. 'Willie had drawn rings round them . . .' and to complete the effect he demonstrated, drawing fast circles round the three names on the paper.

Hackett nodded again. 'So?'

'Well – after I'd er . . .' Bonney hesitated.

'After you'd been caught with your pants down,' Hackett said, hard. 'Yes?'

'Thought I'd do some checking,' Bonney resumed, a touch less breezily. 'Turns out these three ships all belong to the same company: Gulf America Line. And Gulf America . . .' a trace of enjoyment had come back into his voice 'have an office in Jamaica Street. They trade between Antifagasta, Valparaiso, Callao and UK ports: fish-meal, guano, coffee, copper . . .' And this time he really did pause, savouring it.

Hackett looked at him in bored irritation. 'Yeah, well get on with it.'

'And silver,' Bonney said. 'Bullion silver from Callao.'

Hackett was momentarily frozen as he took it in, and Bonney's implication came clear. Bullion silver . . .!

Eventually he asked, 'Any more?'

'I've talked to the Gulf America agent,' Bonney returned, and the enormity of it all was creeping into his own voice now. 'Fella called Latimer. According to him . . .' he prodded at one of the names on the paper, '*Swan Royal* is carrying bullion silver. Half a million quid's worth.'

They looked at one another in the grey, fading light; like testing each other's nerve to believe. Half a million pounds in bullion silver! It was cloud-cuckoo land. And yet, and yet . . .

Hackett went slowly away across the office to switch on the lights. His face was drawn in gaunt lines of disbelief at war with uncertainty, but it was Bonney who broke first.

He said suddenly, 'But they wouldn't would they?' Arguing against his own theory as though acknowledging the craziness of it would knock it on the head so it *couldn't* happen. 'I mean . . . a *ship*?'

'I don't know,' Hackett replied grimly. 'It had to be something big . . . to bring Jouffret.'

They'd drunk too much, all three of them. Throughout the evening Bellis had become progressively more morose and belligerent, while the whisky had honed Jouffret's malice to a fine cutting edge. Their moods had fed off each other. In growing, drink-fuddled dismay Newby had watched his good work of the morning slowly come apart.

This Jouffret was a wicked bastard. The fact that Willie, old bull Willie, was such an easy target had seemed to make him enjoy the baiting all the more, as though he had a compulsive urge to tear to shreds Willie's ego, self-respect, reputation, memories – to destroy it all. There was a viciousness to it that had scared Newby. And it wasn't just a man living up to his reputation; it was something bedded deeper than that, possessing him.

Around nine-thirty Jouffret had suddenly suggested

that they all go back to the docks for a last look. His return flight left first thing in the morning so this was his last chance. Willie had wanted to stay put. After spending damn near all day in and around the docks, if the Frog hadn't seen what he needed to see – too sodding bad! Newby had been aware, for some time, of small, vague ripples of disquiet lapping at nearby tables, so he'd sided with Jouffret; if only to get them out of there, away from the whisky and ears that might catch a careless word. Together he and Jouffret had left Willie with no choice; they'd manhandled him to his feet, taken an arm each and hustled him across the bar. On their way they'd passed Ikey and Cubbon, without even noticing them.

Jouffret had sat in the back of the Jag, whistling some old, French soldier's song. Willie had remained in surly silence, slumped beside Newby where they'd bundled him. Newby had found himself longing for the morning: to be on the motorway, heading home . . . to be back in Chiswick again! He'd thought, 'Sod this for a game of soldiers!' and driven fast, carelessly, not even bothering to check his mirror. Ikey's Dolomite could have been fifty yards closer, sitting right on his tail, and he'd never have known.

They arrived in Jamaica Street just as workers for the flour mills inside the dock were coming on for night shift. Crawling between the straggling groups and past weaving cyclists they looked once more to the Gulf America office, in darkness beyond the railings. Jouffret leaned forward to Willie.

'From here – yes?'

Looking blearily back at him Bellis nodded grudgingly.

'Okay,' the Frenchman said. 'So now you take us on the route, one last time – eh, Willie?' His tone was hard and mocking.

They were lucky with their timing. The sheds and wharves lay deserted at night, and three men in a Jaguar might well have aroused some suspicion in the policeman on the gate: they could hardly have claimed to be off one of the ships – not in a Jag! As it was, the copper was so used to this nightly influx to the mills that he never even bothered to come out of his hut. The Jag rolled safely past, and was in.

Coming over the level crossing behind them Ikey and Cubbon had run into trouble. The Dolomite had got trapped behind an unhurried, straggling wave of men and bikes. Ikey crowded their backs as far as he dare, but the wave was reluctant to break. They'd lost sight of the Jag and were beginning, now, to shoot edgy glances at each other.

Suddenly, with the car still crawling forward, Cubbon threw open his door and dived out. Like running for gold he sprinted the length of the street, weaving and dodging, swerving round bodies and bikes, colliding and stumbling on, not caring about the shouts and laughter at his back. Through the gate he pulled up, heaving, feeling his heart hammering his chest and a burning sensation in his throat. He swung, gazing one way and then the other . . . but there was no sign of the Jag: no sweep of headlights between the sheds, no distant tail lights in the darkness, no broken reflections on the black water.

The Dolomite came through the gates and drew up beside him. Ikey leaned across and opened the passenger door. Still sweating and with a trembling in his legs Cubbon slumped into the seat. 'Lost 'em,' he said bitterly, between gulps for breath. 'We've bloody lost 'em!'

Half a mile away, on an open wharf amidst the clutter of cranes and freight waggons and the long trailers of artics loaded with fruit boxes and machine parts, tea chests or containers, Newby brought the Jag to a halt and switched off the lights. It was quiet here. Across the water were the deck lights of ships, only vaguely discernible against the hard, black bulk of sheds; and further round, the vivid flame of a gas flare above the refinery. But just here there were no lights, and the silence was as deep as the darkness.

After a moment Jouffret said, 'End of the line – eh?'

No one replied. There was another brief pause, then he suddenly kicked open his door and climbed out. He walked a pace or two away from the car and stood staring out over the basin. Newby turned to Bellis looking baffled.

'No good here,' he complained. 'Nowhere to go.'

Bellis shrugged lethargically; he was bored and in a post-booze depression. He couldn't care less. Newby opened his door and followed Jouffret out, calling as he did so, 'No good here, though, is it? Not for a hit. I mean, there's nowhere to bleedin' go!'

Jouffret ignored him. He walked slowly back to the car and opened Willie's door, grinning in at him. 'One thing I don't get . . .' His voice was friendly but puzzled, 'so mebbe you tell me – eh, Willie? . . . If this is as big as we all think – why don't some bastard do it already?'

Willie said bleakly, 'We would 'ave. Harry an' me Six year back . . .' Then he shrugged again. 'We was going to . . . then.'

'No difference,' Jouffret said lightly. 'We do it now, instead. You, Peter an' me.'

Willie shook his head wearily. 'Show you. Said I'd show you . . . An' I 'ave. An' that's it! 'Ow many times 'ave I tole you that? Don't you bloody lissen?'

'Willie . . .' Jouffret said reproachfully.

'Piss off!'

Jouffret reached into the car, took hold of Willie's lapels and dragged him off the seat, in a movement that was so fast and powerful that Willie's knees had hit the concrete before he realised what was happening.

'Hey – bloody hell!' Newby shouted. 'For Christ's sake! . . .'

While Willie was still down Jouffret kicked him in the stomach; then he fell back a pace or two, waiting for him to rise. Willie came up slowly, coughing, using the car to help haul himself back onto his feet. 'You fuckin' bastard!' he said.

Jouffret let it go. 'You listen to me, Willie . . .' he said.

'For Christ's sake!' Newby yelled again.

Jouffret screamed at him, 'Shut up!' He swung back to Willie. 'You're in, Willie, in! So no more – ' he paused, searching for the right word in English, 'bellyaching! You hear? All day you moan, like some old woman! I get sick to hear it!' He was slowly advancing on Willie now, and Willie was retreating, stumbling backwards. 'You know this place, Willie, like . . . your hand – yes? But we don't – so we *need* you. So you're *in*!'

'I've *had* being on blaggin' jobs!' Willie shouted. 'An' no way am I goin' back!'

'Where, back?' Jouffret sneered. He'd caught Willie up now, and was contemptuously prodding him backwards with the flat of his hand.

'He means Parkhurst,' Newby said desperately. 'Prison!'

'What's the matter, Willie?' the Frenchman mocked, prodding him. 'Can't take it?'

'I c'n *do* my bird! . . .'

'He had a bad time there!' Newby shouted. 'That's all.' 'Not goin' back,' Willie repeated. 'Go back – I'll bloody *die* there!'

'No one's going to prison, Willie,' Jouffret laughed.

'How do you know?' Willie yelled. 'Me? I know – 'cos I'm not in! I'm out. Through!'

'You're not listening to me, Willie,' Jouffret shouted over him, 'you should *listen*! . . .' and pushed him again.

Willie heard Newby screaming, 'Jesus! – Watch out!' Then the ground had suddenly run out beneath his feet: the space at his back hurled upwards: the sky was where Jouffret had been . . . and the last thing he heard was his own scream, before the water hit him like a sledgehammer, filling his mouth and nose, and bursting in upon his lungs.

4

It was a Sunday-working docker who found the body. He'd jumped down on to the platform of a floating crane, and was relieving himself over the edge when he saw something in the water below the wharf wall. He realised what it was even before he got there. Willie was floating face-up, utterly still, framed in a murky rainbow of oil. His face was bloated, blue, grey, and empty. It was eight-thirty a.m. He'd been in the water for over ten hours.

By eight-thirty-five the Dock Police had arrived, and boat hooks were raking over Willie's chest, hauling him in. It was at exactly the same time as Jouffret, at the airport, was boarding a Paris-bound One-Eleven, and if Willie was anywhere in his thoughts it didn't show. The hard face was as contained and impassive as ever, betraying nothing.

And by that time, also, Newby was on the motorway, putting distance behind him. He still felt vaguely numb, with a confused sensation of sick anger that came over him in waves. He'd tried to save Willie, but by the time he'd got down the iron ladder to where the rungs were wet, the thrashing in the water had stopped.

It wasn't so much the demise of Willie Bellis for Willie's own sake that now sickened him; hell, what was Willie except an over-the-hill slag with BO? But killing him had to be pure bloody stupidity, because if the cops suspected foul play then this whole sodding caper was blown; and Jouffret should have thought of that, only he hadn't, because Jouffret was a madman! That worried him too, gnawed at him, the thought of being alongside that unpredictable bastard on the job, and Jouffret all tooled up with a loaded shotgun. It was enough to keep you awake nights, was that. Mustn't ever let the Frenchman get behind him, he thought; never turn his back.

A small blue sign at the side of the motorway told him that London was seventy-three miles away. He pressed his foot harder on the accelerator, longing to be home.

As chance would have it, while Newby was burning rubber on the motorway, Hackett was less than a mile from where Willie's body was lying, though news of it hadn't as yet reached him. He was with Latimer, the Gulf America agent, who was giving up his Sunday morning to drive him around the docks. Latimer didn't hugely mind. He'd have been trying to get his youngest ready for church round about this time, and that was a weekly war of wills he was happy to leave to his wife for a change.

He was an easy-going, friendly man in his middle forties. His contact with the police – other than the Dock Police with most of whom he was on first-name terms – had, up to now, been minimal. His contact with crime had been nil. His house had never been burgled, his car stolen or his wallet pinched. He'd never witnessed a robbery, or an assault, or even served on a jury. So it was taking him some time to come to terms with the idea that, if Hackett was right, a group of armed criminals were planning to come into the docks to steal half a million pounds' worth of silver bullion. He had that incredulity of the innocent which Hackett found faintly tedious.

'Half a million?' the agent had said. 'But it couldn't be done!'

And Hackett had replied grimly, 'We know some who might try.'

Even so, Latimer was still finding it difficult to be convinced, but was glad enough to explain to Hackett the arrangements for the silver; because those were fact, easy, and tended he thought, anyway, to substantiate his scepticism.

'At Callao it's loaded in wooden boxes into the Special Cargo Locker. Sheet steel doors, welded shut . . .'

'Welded?'

Latimer nodded. 'At Callao. So the only way to get the silver out, when the ship docks, is to burn the lock off with an oxy-acetylene torch.'

'Who does that?'

'Shoreside people . . . but the First Officer has charge. Then they load the silver into a cargo net, sling it over the side, and into a truck.'

'Security firm?'

Latimer nodded again. 'But they use a plain truck, so's not to attract attention.'

'That's what they're going to hit,' Hackett said confidently, and Latimer shook his head in bemused incredulity. One had only got to think of what the damn stuff weighed, for God's sake! But that didn't seem to be bothering Hackett. In fact, there was only one small thing still niggling him: Willie had marked three ships, and the *Swan Royal* was only one of them. When he asked Latimer about the others, *Swan Hunter* and *Swan*

Castle, the agent shrugged. They weren't carrying anything worth an armed robbery. The only thing they had in common with *Swan Royal* was that they were due to dock on the same tide, which was rare enough these days: for a company to have three of its ships arriving in one port more or less simultaneously; happened perhaps twice a year – if that.

So why did he think Willie had ringed them, Hackett asked.

'Maybe, at the time, he wasn't sure which one was carrying the silver,' Latimer hazarded, then realised with a rueful grin that now he, too, was subscribing to the bullion theory.

'Where are you when the silver comes ashore?' Hackett asked.

'Paying off the crew. Day or two out the ship radios what cash she'll need. Once she's docked I take it aboard and the deep-sea crew pays off; then the coasting crew comes aboard.'

'So you don't go with the silver?'

Latimer laughed and shook his head. 'By the time I'm through that's stashed behind time-locks and steel bars – some vault in the city.'

Hackett smiled grimly. 'Not if these merchants get their way,' he said.

Passing grain elevators and freight sidings, sheds and warehouses, they were now heading towards the wharf alongside which, in six days' time, the *Swan Royal* would be docking. A minute or two before a police unit-beat car had overtaken them and gone racing ahead. Hackett hadn't paid it much attention. But now, also overtaking them, came a second police car followed by a black van. It didn't register with Latimer but Hackett knew it for what it was: an undertaker's vehicle. With a small mental jolt that came very near to some kind of premonition, he said urgently, 'Follow them, will you.'

'No choice,' Latimer returned, still unaware. 'No place for them to go from here, 'cept the same place we're going.'

Sure enough, as they turned on to the wide, open wharf they could see the two police cars parked behind the van, and a small, drab huddle of figures close by the edge, waiting almost motionless, hunched against the wind in the bleak, grey light.

Recalling it at a later date Hackett would swear that he'd known what he was going to see even before he got out of the car. But whether that was also before he consciously recognised the tall, black-garbed figure of the Reverend, he couldn't be sure.

Griffiths was standing a little apart, hands buried in his coat pockets, head bowed, staring down to the water. He heard the slamming of car doors and footsteps at his back, then words blown out like candles guttering in the wind. He recognised one of the voices and turned. Hackett was kneeling beside Willie's body, lifting away the shabby, sodden raincoat from the dead face. After a pause he let it drop again and stood slowly. His glance came up to meet Griffiths', and for a bleak moment their eyes were locked over the poor earthly remains of Willie Bellis.

'My name and address on a letter in his pocket,' Griffiths said eventually. 'Virtually all he had on him – that . . .' He paused briefly as the wind stung his eyes, making them water; or perhaps as the wide, deep river of sorrow inside him, that ran always to the infinite ocean of God's mercy, briefly burst its banks, at the futility of Willie's life and the waste of his death and that this was where and how it should end. 'So they . . . came to tell me,' he continued, struggling. 'Brought me back with them.'

'This isn't the way I wanted it,' Hackett said awkwardly.

'This is the way you've got it, though!' the Reverend replied bitterly.

'When we take the others – they'll answer for this as much as the rest.'

'And all the choirs of God's angels will sing at your bloody back, boy!'

Griffiths turned away angrily and stood staring at the gulls wheeling over the scummy water, and the almost lazy-seeming movement of crane jibs across the dock.

Hackett gave him a moment to see whether he'd turn again, but the massive back was shut hard against him like a door in his face. 'Take it,' he said eventually in cold retaliation, 'take it, you're identifying him – official?'

Without turning Griffiths said, 'Should be his wife, to do that.'

'She was years ago,' Hackett said contemptuously. 'Took it on her toes years ago.'

'Well, she's back now,' Griffiths flared at him. He paused a moment, as though debating whether to tell Hackett or not, then he said, 'Not much cop your Intelligence system, is it? I know where she is. Went to see her once – for Willie: though he didn't know it. And a good thing, too; for she had about as much charity in her unhappy soul – poor, bloody cow as you, boy bach!'

The bitterness of the words was lost on Hackett. He was too preoccupied with a sense of dull shock. That she'd come back . . . dared to come back! He wondered again whether Willie ever knew who it was who'd stitched him. Not that it mattered much now, because Willie was dead. But again there was that eroding disgust inside him, like acid in his stomach, and if only in vindictive malice he knew now what there was to do.

'Ought to tell her she's a widow,' he said.

'Not me.' Griffiths shook his head and looked briefly back to the screaming gulls. 'Owe her nothing.'

'No. But she owes me,' Hackett returned evenly.

'Did he fall? Or was he pushed?' Tate asked. It wasn't an original question, but it was pertinent.

He was standing with Hackett on the small jetty at the yacht club. The estuary lay grey and choppy under a dull grey sky, with a slicing wind that came off the sea like the repeated slash of a scythe. Not many yachts were out – just a few coloured sails tacking and running, or lying into the wind beyond the mud banks: little blurs of red and orange and blue against the sky. Hackett shivered as he thought how cold it must be out there, shivered because it was bitter enough just standing here.

Tate's face was stung red with spray and his windcheater was patched with dark areas of wet. Hackett had known this was where he'd find him, his Sunday playground, all year through. Tate was an all-weather yachtsman. Outside policing it was virtually his only passion.

'Either,' Hackett said with a shrug. 'Or a bit of both. Been enough aggro between them for it to be murder. Or manslaughter, anyway.'

'But you don't want the coroner to know that,' Tate said pensively.

'Don't want it said in court,' Hackett corrected him.

'Why?' Tate was playing devil's advocate. He knew damn well why. But he was going to make Hackett justify himself; and justify whatever vaguely improper suggestion he wanted to put to the coroner, or whatever half-truths were going to be told that Tate might be asked to substantiate.

'Blow the operation,' Hackett said simply. 'We get a verdict of murder – or even manslaughter – brought in . . . Newby and Jouffret are going to know the place is crawling. Won't show their faces anywhere near.'

'What makes you think there's still an operation to be blown?' Tate persisted. 'Now Willie's dead maybe that's killed the whole caper.'

'No way!' Hackett returned, almost shouting against the wind. 'They're going for the big one – half a million! No way they're going to cry off just because of Willie.'

'Although they've gone, haven't they? Back where they came from.'

'The *Swan Royal* doesn't dock for six days. And they've got soldiers to recruit.'

Tate stood a moment staring at the smattering of sails on the water, half his mind with them out there, the other half gently turning over what Hackett was wanting done. He respected Hackett for being a tough, dedicated and clever copper, but sometimes the way Hackett had run operations had come perilously close to the inadmissible: something of the cowboy about him that had to be watched. His teeth chattering Hackett waited, wishing they could get off the jetty and out of this wind; but until they'd finished talking shop he knew there could be no move for the crowded bar.

'Not up to me, up to Benson,' Tate said eventually. 'But he won't like it.'

Benson was the coroner. On occasions in the past he'd clearly demonstrated that he didn't necessarily see any correlation between his pursuit of truth and Hackett's pursuit of justice. What's more, as the senior partner in a firm of solicitors in the city there had been one occasion, five years before, when he and Hackett had fallen badly foul of each other. Hackett had accused one of Benson's clients of starting the fire that had destroyed his timber yard business; to rip off the insurance, had been Hackett's contention. Not long afterwards the city police had caught a pyromaniac who'd confessed to the timber yard fire as well as several others.

Charges had been withdrawn against Benson's client and Hackett had apologised; but a letter of complaint had gone to the Chief Constable, and if Benson had had his way and his client hadn't been nearly such a broken man, almost certainly there'd have been a suit for wrongful arrest.

'Doesn't like me much,' Hackett confessed.

'Better ask him nicely then, hadn't you?'

'Rather hoped you might,' Hackett suggested casually.

Tate laughed as though he'd know that was coming. 'Don't want me stomping all over your operation, do you, Steve?'

'Back me, then.'

'Always do, you know that.'

'So I can say it's as much from you as from me.'

Tate paused again, reflecting. 'Depends what you're going to ask him for. And that you are going to *ask*, and not try to *tell* him, you know?' Hackett looked away angrily, resenting the implication. 'I can't afford to be party to an out-and-out lie, Steve, so he'll have to be told the lot. Cards on the table, right?'

It wasn't the way Hackett had been intending to play it – not quite. But now he had no choice but to nod reluctantly, resigned.

'Means you won't get "accidental death",' Tate continued, 'not once he knows they were seen arguing, so no point in asking. You might get him to agree to adjourn *sine die*, though, waiting for further medical evidence – something like that.' He looked evenly at Hackett. 'Best I can think of. Worth trying, anyway.' He half-turned and looked towards the clubhouse beyond the slipway, through a lattice of sloping masts where dinghies were beached, listing slightly, and the wind strummed their wires and played percussion on their tarpaulins. 'Let's have that drink,' he said abruptly, and began at last to move away from the jetty.

Hackett stayed where he was. A sense of angry frustration was slowly burgeoning inside him. He couldn't stop seeing Willie's face the way it had been, in death, on that cold wharf. Like something that had been thrown away – obsolete. It played peek-a-boo in his memory with the face of that other Willie, bellowing in sick rage. That was when Willie had stopped being the man he once was, and had started down the path that ended in the choking black water of the dock. And because he felt partly responsible for that, for having let himself be used by Harry and Willie's wife, for having allowed Willie to play once more in a league he was too old and too punchy to handle, Hackett's determination to stitch Newby and Jouffret – for life! – had become an imperative. No one, not even upright Mr Benson, could be allowed to get in the way of that.

Tate paused and looked back. The wind was whipping Hackett's hair. He was standing doggedly still, gazing over the estuary, hard and unyielding.

'You coming?' Tate called.

Hackett looked towards him, but made no move to join him, and Tate could see the blackness flowering in his face.

'I want those bastards!' Hackett shouted. 'In six days I want them back here! Doing what I *know* they'll be doing!' He started slowly to move towards Tate. 'So I can lift them!'

'You make it sound as though I don't!' Tate called back.

Hackett ignored him. 'They killed Willie even if they didn't push him,' he continued. 'So once we've got them for the other thing we can try to nail that on them too! But we're just pissing into the wind unless we get them for the other thing first!'

'Don't shout at me, Steve!'

Hackett pulled up and checked his outburst. For a moment they were glaring at each other. Calmer, he said, 'We all know how Willie died: he drowned.'

'Not had the PM yet, have we?'

'Odds on, though – drowned. So what someone's got to make Benson realise, what he'd got to be *told* . . . is that how it happened doesn't bloody matter – not like sewing up those other two bastards matters. Does it?!'

It seemed an age before Tate replied. He nodded abruptly. 'Then it better had be me who talks to Benson after all,' he said. 'You don't go near him – understood?'

Hackett nodded, only dimly beginning to perceive that he'd won.

'Can't do anything today because it's Sunday, you know?' Tate continued sarcastically. 'Have to be first thing in the morning. Do for you?'

Hackett nodded again, and managed a wry grin.

'Only one thing,' Tate said quietly. 'When you get me begging favours for you – you owe me: first, that you're not wrong; and second, that you don't screw anything up!'

Hackett wasn't sure how serious he was being. 'No, sir,' he said, with exaggerated tolerance.

Louise turned off the broad, sweeping road that bound in the houses like a concrete moat, and drove towards the heart of the estate. It had to be, she thought, the last place God made; or the finest example of some housing planner's inhumanity.

It was set on a high plateau above the city, and possibly its one half-redeeming feature was the view. From the perimeter road one could see clear across woods beyond the river to the rich grazing of farmland below hills that were purple and hazy with distance. The nearest woods were a patchwork of greens, oranges, yellows and browns, although in the dull afternoon light the colours lacked lustre; were almost drab. Further round was the broadening expanse of estuary, grey, and flecked with white where it opened to the sea. Then came the sprawling lie of the city that seemed to stretch for ever, overcast with fumes and the smoke of industry.

The estate itself was built all in concrete blocks, row after row of grey, ugly semis, featureless and chilling. Every house was the same. The gardens were all in the same state of sad abandonment: rank patches of grass, weed-filled borders and privet hedges that had never known the discipline of shears. Every street was the same in its sense of barren despair. There were no trees, no people even. It was utterly quiet and deserted: a flat, grey, wind-swept ghetto.

There was one building Louise passed that was standing alone, like a giant, grey blockhouse set in the middle of a scraggy, cratered patch of open ground. Around it, amidst the chick-weed and nettles and parched, coarse grass, were littered the rusting frames of bicycles, a pram, an old gas oven, and the carcass of a car. Louise saw a scarred board outside the padlocked doors: bingo hall; cinema on Sunday nights only. It was the one amenity that had been provided. Showing that night was 'Emmanuelle 2'.

After driving around for nearly a quarter of an hour Louise found the street she wanted, empty and forlorn as the rest. She parked outside one of the houses and walked slowly up the cracked path towards the front door. Along the street the rest of the houses watched blindly. The absence of even one twitching curtain, coupled with the windy silence, was faintly unnerving. She rapped the chrome door knocker that was pitted with rust.

Half a minute – possibly more – passed, and she knocked again – twice. Then, dimly, she thought she detected movement on the other side of the door. There was the sound of a lock being unlatched and the door swung open. A woman was standing there.

'Mrs Bellis?' Louise enquired coolly.

And the woman nodded, slowly.

Evie Bellis: widow of this parish; last stop before hell.

But she wasn't the woman Hackett had described; not at all the woman she once was. Oh – Louise could tell she'd been a looker, once; nothing could destroy the bone structure of the face, or the sensuality of the mouth, or even the faintly arrogant line of the nose. But these were like the last defenders of ground that was already lost: the remainder of her looks were long gone – to fat, and folds of sagging flesh.

She must have been in her early forties, Louise guessed, still too young to look as old as she did. She'd lost her figure, had become too thick around the middle, too large all over. And anyway, it couldn't be just age, Louise was thinking: for God's sake, it was only six years ago she'd run off with Harry, so she must still have had some looks then. Wearing a cheap, tawdry dress with the roots of her hair showing dark, Evie stood there in the half-open door, waiting. And it came to Louise quite suddenly: she was looking at a woman who'd simply stopped caring, and who'd let herself go.

'My name's Colbert,' Louise said. 'Detective Sergeant.' And held out her warrant card for Evie to read.

There was a brief flicker of astonishment on Evie's face, then the expression settled into well-practised lines of contempt, still remembered from the good, old days. 'My God,' she said, and laughed.

'May I come in for a moment?'

'I don't mind us talkin' out 'ere, Flower. Not like you're in uniform, is it?'

'Only I'm afraid I have some bad news to give you.'

That threw Evie slightly. She hesitated, but when she saw that Louise wasn't going to say any more unless she came inside Evie grudgingly moved to let her pass. 'I was sittin' in the back,' she said; and Louise could smell the drink on her breath now.

The room at the back was adjacent to a cubby-hole kitchen and was obviously where she spent most – if not all – of her time. It was furnished very nearly as a bed-sitter, seeming to suggest that she'd reduced all of living to what could be accommodated in this small space. It was crammed with furniture, all of it old and none of it matching.

There was a vinyl-topped table bearing the remains of an out-of-a-packet meal; a couple of armchairs in front of the gas fire – both needing re-covering; a sideboard along one wall, littered on top with piles of cheap paperback thrillers, magazines, her open handbag lying on its side spewing its contents, one or two small, badly tarnished silver cups with a ballroom dancing couple engraved on them, and finally a photograph of Evie herself, at least ten years younger. Looking at it Louise understood very clearly how it must have been between her and men: looking like that they'd not have left her alone; and looking like that – she'd not have wanted them to.

But not any more. Now there were different pleasures. In one corner was a divan she was using as a settee. On a table beside it was an open box of chocolates, and a half-empty bottle of whisky. Briefly Louise wondered whether they were her compensations, new pleasures to replace the old; or had the new pleasures come first and started the rot?

Opposite the divan was a television – black and white –

showing an old western. but with the sound turned right down; while on the table beside the chocolates was a transistor radio playing pop music. It gave Louise a small, unpleasant jolt seeing the TV was on; there was something off-balance and unhealthy here; like the fact, also, that the heavy curtains were drawn shut, and the room was lit only by a dull-shining table lamp perched on the end of the sideboard.

Louise turned. 'Your husband . . .' she said, and hesitated.

'Willie? . . .' There was clear surprise in Evie's voice.

'William Archer Bellis – yes?'

'Bloody silly name for a puddin' like Willie.'

'He's dead, Mrs Bellis.'

There was only the briefest of pauses, then Evie started casually across towards the divan. If she was moved or surprised she wasn't showing it. And she was holding her drink well, Louise thought, still retaining almost complete mastery of her legs. She flopped on to the divan and replenished her glass from the bottle. 'How?' she asked at length, but sounding only mildly curious.

'He drowned. In the docks.'

'In the docks?' She looked surprised again. 'Didn't know he was out.' She sipped her whisky. 'Drowned? . . . He would.' She looked at Louise and smiled. 'Don't wanna look so solemn, Flower. Not like the end o' the worl', is it?'

Despite knowing what Evie had done six years ago and that, consequently, she shouldn't be surprised, Louise couldn't help feeling slightly sickened by the woman's reaction. 'They think he was drunk,' she said coldly, eyeing Evie's glass.

'Where'd 'e get the money for tha', then?' was Evie's only response.

Before she bit it back Louise almost said, 'Same place

you get yours, I should imagine.' Instead she said, 'There's the matter of identification.'

Evie burst into laughter, and some of the whisky slopped out of the glass down the front of her dress as she shook. 'Me? . . .' She licked her fingers where the whisky had run. 'Don't know as I c'n remember wha' 'e looked like, now. 'Aven't seen 'im in over six year . . . Course, you'll know why.'

'Too bloody right!' Louise thought sourly, but her face remained perfectly impassive. 'You're the only living relative,' she persisted calmly.

She wasn't trying to con Evie: she genuinely believed that formal identification had still to be made, because somehow Hackett had forgotten to mention that the Reverend had already obliged. In fact, what he'd said was, 'Tell her he's dead, then get her down to the mortuary to identify the body.' So whatever game he was playing, Louise wasn't in on it.

Evie knocked back the remainder of the whisky in her glass, but didn't put it down. She held it, letting her glance drift back to the bottle. 'Not juss now, Flower,' she said, and a hard edge had come into her tone.

'It won't take very long,' Louise said evenly.

'Juss gettin' into this film, aren' I?' She was reaching for the bottle again.

Very calmly Louise walked deliberately across to the silent, flickering screen and switched it off. Then she stood facing Evie, staring her out.

'Bleedin' cow,' Evie said.

Hackett was waiting for them when they arrived at the mortuary. Louise had radioed her movements in to the office while they were on their way. Now, coming through the heavy double doors with frosted-glass panels into the cool of the chamber, they saw him talking to the attendant half way down the bank of steel drawers that were like the drawers of some giant filing cabinet. One of these, close beside the two men, had been drawn out and on its slab they could see a white sheet draped over the dead bulk of a body.

Hackett turned as they approached, and at that moment Evie recognised him.

'Hello, Evie,' he said.

She stopped abruptly. Despite the dark glasses she was wearing the shock was clearly written on her face. Her mouth had opened but no sound came out. She stood momentarily transfixed, gaping foolishly. Louise was half-expecting her to turn round and walk right back out again, but either she hadn't got the presence of mind or was too gutsy for that. Instead she started to walk slowly forward once more.

'Thanks for coming,' Hackett said.

She stopped beside the open drawer and took off her dark glasses, appraising him in cool, undisguised contempt. 'Should've known, shouldn' I?' she said eventually. 'Bit like a bad penny – you, Mister Hackett.'

'Where Willie goes – there go I,' Hackett returned pleasantly.

'All the way, I 'ope,' she replied.

Hackett smiled, unperturbed. 'Only heard you were back recently. How've you been keeping?'

'Didn't come for no social, Mister Hackett,' she said. 'Didn't wanna come at all on'y she,' nodding insolently towards Louise, 'bloody made me. Your idea, was it?'

He nodded, smiling.

'Thought so,' she said. 'Anyways, seein' now I'm 'ere . . .' She looked at the attendant and nodded to the shrouded figure. 'That 'im?'

The attendant looked towards Hackett who gave a small nod of assent. The man bent forward and lifted the sheet at the near end of the drawer, pulling it back to reveal the head and shoulders of Willie Bellis. Evie paused a moment, steeling herself, then looked down.

Willie's face wasn't the way she remembered it: it was coarser, flabbier, older. She was faintly disgusted by it. It awoke in her only the dimmest of – not even memories, but sensations that were confused and unsettling: contempt mingling with bitterness mingling with guilt mingling with anger. The drink was still not completely cleared from her brain so her defences were impaired. She could feel herself becoming upset for reasons she couldn't grasp, and like bubbles of air churning up through water there came great gobs of self-pity rising to the surface of her confusion.

'Mrs Bellis, do you know this man?' Louise was formally asking.

'Don't bother,' Hackett said.

Evie turned away without answering.

'Mrs Bellis, do you know who . . .' Louise persisted, but Hackett cut her short.

'She knows damn well who it is.'

'She's got to say so,' Louise almost shouted at him.

'All right – yes! That's Willie!' Evie said bitterly.

'We know,' Hackett said. 'He's already been identified. I just thought you might like to see him.'

'What? . . .' Louise said vaguely.

Evie was looking at Hackett with pure hate on her face. 'The chaplain to the prison identified him this morning,' he continued calmly. 'But I thought you'd want to see him one last time, Evie.'

'Bleedin' bastard!' she said.

'They'll be cutting him up tomorrow,' Hackett rode on remorselessly, determined to twist the knife and have *same* satisfaction from her. 'And burning him the day after. So you have a last look to remember him by.'

'Sir!' Louise said, shocked.

'Six years inside,' he said, the disgust of all those years larding his voice, 'ten days out. Then *that*. So you have another look, Evie.'

'Why don't you!?' Evie returned. 'You nicked him! Only too happy to feel 'is collar!'

'And I'd do it again,' Hackett said. 'But I'd not be used again, not by the likes of you and Harry. Now why don't you take another look, Evie, and tell me whether Harry was worth *that*!'

'Sir!' Louise pleaded.

Hackett ignored her. He was going to demolish Evie. He'd waited too long for this. 'Not with you now, is he? So how many years did he give you? Or months! Were they really worth *that*?'

'Harry didn't leave me,' Evie cried back. 'Not really leave me! Juss I didn't wanna live in France! Thassall! 'E said 'e 'ad to so's you lot couldn't touch 'im, but I didn't wanna live in bloody France, did I? If 'e 'adn't 'ad to we'd've been together now!'

Looking at the woman Louise knew it had to be a delusion that her tatty self-respect demanded; and she didn't know whether to laugh or cry. Briefly she was almost sorry for her: and furious with Hackett who had no right to bait her, not like this . . .

Unrelenting, he was continuing savagely, 'How long did Willie's six years buy you, Evie?'

'Two years!' she flung back at him. 'We 'ad two good years!'

And Hackett started to laugh – at the monstrosity of it all: six years' dying for two years on the town! What a deal! What a . . . Then, very abruptly, he stopped as it hit him; and he felt almost numb with the shock of it. Evie had just given him one piece of the jigsaw he'd never even realised existed . . . and it was the key piece, that held the whole picture together!

'Harry went to France?' he said sharply.

She was thrown by the change of tack. She managed to nod, floundering.

'Is he still there?'

'Where you can't touch 'im!'

'Of course . . .' he thought. 'Of *course*!'

Louise hadn't caught on yet. She was looking at Hackett in bewilderment. But she had to wait – he made her wait – until they were leaving and Evie, going on ahead, was out of earshot. Then, in a kind of triumph, he said quietly, 'What Jouffret is, is just the link-man . . . don't you see?'

5

It was like a scab being scraped from a festering wound, this rubbing raw of an old obsession. There was pus in the wound; it had a name; it was called Harry Smith. And it allowed Hackett no sleep that night.

It allowed him no repose of any kind. It kept him on the move through all the cramped rooms of his flat, bedroom to living-room to hallway and back, unable to settle anywhere. He tried perching on chairs or the edge of his bed but always the mental riot forced him up and to move again; and he prowled neurotically through midnight into morning. He brewed himself coffee; played Janis Joplin on his stereo; and kept on moving through the softly lit space of his rooms while his mind bled, oozing pus.

Smith: the last of all that bad team. Smith: the one

he'd never caught. Smith: now residing in France where the British police couldn't touch him. And Evie had been right about that: damn Harry to hell and back, he'd known what he was about, known that the French would not extradite him for the crime of conspiracy. And that was all – *all*? – Harry had done: conspired with others – with William Archer Bellis, and with Frank Steen and Victor Lawson, Michael Nolan, Tony Lorraine and Charles Henry Bates – conspired with them to commit robbery, and assault with intent to commit robbery. Only while his team had pulled the stunts Harry had sat at home like a fat cat.

Not like a fat cat, Hackett thought. That wasn't being fair to Harry. There wasn't anything fat or sleek or lazy about him. Harry was the hardest of them all; the best! Hard and clever and lacking in any scruples, devoid of all morality, Harry was a criminal because that was all he wanted to be: utterly criminal because, as a man, there was no other way he could be.

He'd been responsible for jobs – to Hackett's certain knowledge – worth over a million. For three years, when Willie was with him, they'd had a job away damn near every week. Once, in a single job, they'd pulled ninety thousand in notes. That was the calibre of the men they were, before Hackett and the likes of Hackett had sniped them off, one by one: men to be reckoned with.

Which Harry still was, but he was safe, and it galled Hackett. The only small satisfaction he could find was the thought of what Harry's life must have become to force him to cut and run. He must have known that nothing – luck, success, immunity – could last for ever. His card was marked. And no matter how careful he was, how many cut-outs he used, how scrupulously he avoided using any phone with which he was known to be associated and might, therefore, be tapped, he must have known he was living on borrowed time. With malicious relish Hackett thought of the ever-increasing precautions Harry must have taken, the anxiety filling his days and his dreams, all the complicated arrangements just to keep himself safe . . . until, one day, he must have weighed his life in the balance and known he was already in a kind of prison. And with so many small slips waiting to be made it could only be a question of time before he found himself in a real one. So he'd taken it on his toes, leaving England and Evie behind him, and gone to France where Hackett, and the likes of Hackett, couldn't touch him.

Only now, from the safety of France, Harry was going back into business, recruiting again, organising a hit worth half a million.

Hackett wanted to believe that, as much as he wanted to believe that Willie was dead because Jouffret had pushed him. Otherwise . . . there were enough bloody coincidences here to confound the best mathematician in the business! Harry had gone to France – yes! Was still there – so far as Evie knew, though she'd said she didn't know where he was living and Hackett had believed her. But a hard man called Jouffret, who was just the calibre of man Harry would choose, had come all the way from France to meet with Willie Bellis, Harry's one-time friend and soldier. So this caper in the docks had to be a Harry Smith operation. Lifting half a million in silver bullion, what's more – that was just the calibre of job one should expect of Harry, bent bastard of a genius that he was!

Physical tiredness was beginning to slow Hackett down. He felt himself growing colder as his metabolic rate dropped towards the body's low point around three a.m. But still his mind wouldn't stop its acrobatics, turning the theory in cartwheels and somersaults, over and over, testing it this way and that, in order to be sure it was truly sound, and not just the blindness of obsession.

Harry – France – Jouffret – Willie – back to Harry again. It looked so perfect he almost cherished it. And yet . . . with weary reluctance he was forced to acknowledge that there were weaknesses. Why had Willie died? Accident? As a result of the argument with Jouffret? Or because he was a threat to them? But how could he have been? Or because he'd refused to play ball? But why should he have? Unless, maybe . . . and Hackett was almost unwilling to admit the thought because, if it was true, it played havoc with his whole thesis: suppose Willie had known about Evie and Harry! That would have made him a less than enthusiastic member. But had he known? That Evie had gone – certainly: but had he known with whom?

They tormented Hackett, these questions without answers. They were like the soft, vulnerable underbelly of his argument, where the skinning could begin. If Willie *had* known, he argued back against himself, then no way would Harry have recruited him again. And in any case, Willie wouldn't have answered the call . . .

And round and round he went, till he was almost dizzy with the strain of it, trying to find one clear, unassailable strand of logic buried in the midst of too many unknown quantities; and fighting the tiredness that was beginning to fog his brain. By the time he knew it was useless to go on trying to fight it, he'd still got no further. He could only hold to those possibilities which allowed him to believe what he wanted to believe: that Willie had never known who it was Evie had gone with; had answered Harry's call like the faithful, old dog he was; had died stupidly and unnecessarily; and what was planned to happen in six days' time was a genuine, hallmarked, Harry Smith operation.

Across his curtains, on the outside, he noticed a greyness that was new. He stood quite still, listening, and could hear the low hum of his stereo that had stopped playing, unnoticed, hours ago. Then, very briefly, there was the trill of a bird, just one phrase that ended abruptly almost as though the bird had surprised itself. Hackett stood in blank, drained astonishment: not dawn! He couldn't have been prowling all through the night! . . . His watch told him it was nearly five-thirty.

Slowly he began to realise just how dreadful he felt. There was a leadenness all over his body, and such coldness inside him he was shivering in spasms. When he moved it was as though everything was happening in slow motion. He felt physically dirty, itchy, and his eyes were stiff with tiredness.

Outside the bird trilled again, this time longer, and was met by an answering call. A car passed in the street. Monday-bloody-Monday, Hackett thought. Now there were just five clear days before the *Swan Royal* would be docking. He groaned. In slow motion he moved through his bedroom and stood a moment staring balefully at his bed. Too late for that now; too much to do. Shivering, feeling tender as though he was starting with 'flu, he stripped off his clothes, leaving them littering the floor, and went to shower.

As the hot water streamed over him he felt warmth coming back to his body. He turned his face to the rose as a man who'd been trapped underground might turn his face to the sun, and basked in it, feeling the weariness slowly recede and new life coming into him. It wasn't any real compensation for lack of sleep but it made him feel human again; and by the time he stepped out of the shower and began almost brutally to towel himself, he knew what had to be done: he had to prove his theory was right, before Saturday next, *prove* that Harry was back at work again.

It was mid-morning before Tate got into the office. Benson, the Coroner, hadn't exactly given him an easy time. God knows what sort of a time he'd have given Hackett, Tate thought. Only after a lot of talking, a lot of persuasion, had Benson agreed to co-operate, and then only on a limited basis. But it was enough.

The main office was busy this morning. About a dozen detectives were in, clustered in twos and threes, or sitting at desks reading files, writing reports or glued to phones scribbling notes. There was an animated buzz of voices. Phones were constantly ringing. It had the kind of atmosphere of a small newspaper office on press day, the same kind of controlled chaos: piles of paper strewn everywhere, chairs left at odd angles where they'd been vacated in a hurry, the faint haze of cigarette smoke, plastic coffee cups abandoned half-full. Overall there was a feeling of vitality which Tate enjoyed.

Only Hackett looked anything but vital. Stopping at his door Tate experienced a mild sense of shock. Hackett looked lousy: pasty-faced with purple-black shadows under his eyes, and a heavy, drooping quality to the way he sat.

'Word with you?' Tate said, nodding towards his own office.

'Waiting for a call, sir,' Hackett said, indicating the phone.

Tate moved on into the office and closed the door. Hackett lumbered to his feet, gestured to a chair and waited for Tate to sit. Then he slumped again. Whenever he moved or spoke it was like a delayed reaction, as though his brain was only working on half revs.

'Heavy night?' Tate asked.

Hackett shook his head. 'Just never managed to get any sleep.'

'Should tell her how old you really are, Steve; then

maybe she'd not make so many demands on you.'

Hackett gave his boss a tired, indulgent smile.

'Talked to Benson,' Tate resumed. 'And he didn't like it . . . but he'll play ball for a week: adjourn *sine die* for a week. Long enough, I hope. Have to be, won't it?'

'Long enough,' Hackett said. 'As long as they're not scared off between now and Saturday – that's all I want.' His phone rang and he picked it up. 'Superintendent Hackett . . .'

It was the girl on the switchboard. 'Call from France for you, sir.'

'Right, thanks.' He covered the mouthpiece and said to Tate, 'Lou got on to the French again this morning. Asked them to run another tracer on Jouffret for us.'

'Why?' Tate said. 'Thought we knew all about him.'

'Yeah, but it's got more complicated. Tell you in a minute.' On the other end of the phone, through the customary frying of eggs, he could hear a man's voice saying, 'Allô . . . allô . . .'

'Allô,' Hackett said. 'Ca c'est Commissaire Vatan?'

'Oui . . .'

'Allô, M'sieur, je suis Hackett, Detective Superintendent Hackett – er, du bureau des operations – er . . . au sud Angleterre . . .'

He heard Tate starting to laugh, at his French, he supposed, but he didn't have time to retaliate because the voice at the other end of the phone, although still Vatan's, had suddenly become startlingly comprehendable. 'Allô, M'sieur – per'aps it would be better if I talk English – I don' mind.'

Hackett felt a sense of relief that was tinged with embarrassment. 'Oh!' he said, 'yes, thank you . . . Er – my, er . . . my Detective Sergeant speaks French very well, but I – er . . .'

'I don' mind,' Vatan repeated. 'I only 'ope I can be

understood.'

'Perfectly, M'sieur.'

'Alors. Your Mam'selle Colbert asked about – Roland Jouffret, this man you are . . .'

'That's right,' Hackett interrupted.

'Roland Jouffret – we know. We 'ad 'oped, per'aps, we might be lucky and 'e wouldn' come back, you know?' This was accompanied by a light, dry laugh.

'Do I take it he is back?'

'Last night.'

'In Bruay?'

'At the 'Otel Boule d'Or.'

'I see . . .' Hackett paused briefly to think, and wasn't in the best condition for it. Jouffret was back in Bruay – that was good. So what next? Next . . . he had to contact Harry: if Hackett's theory was right, sometime or other they had to meet. And if Jouffret was back already, odds on that still hadn't happened – which was even better.

Vatan was saying, ' 'Allo, are you still there, M'sieur?'

'Yes – sorry,' Hackett said. 'I was just trying to think.'

'Oh – but yes: often I 'ave the same problem,' Vatan responded drily.

With a weak grin Hackett said, 'M'sieur . . . I'm hoping I may be able to come to Bruay personally . . .'

'Pardon? . . . You intend to come 'ere yourself?'

'Tonight or tomorrow – yes.' As he spoke Hackett was looking at Tate and was aware of a change in his boss's face. It was becoming hard and closed. He looked away and carried on quickly, 'It would be very helpful to me if we could meet.'

There was an appreciable pause at the other end. Vatan had obviously been thrown. Eventually the Frenchman said, 'Would this visit . . . be an official one, M'sieur?'

'Not official,' Hackett said carefully. He didn't know

how hidebound by convention or protocol Vatan might be, but 'official' meant channels and clearances and politics: 'official' could take for ever and he didn't have the time. 'Too . . . rigid,' he said, 'too complicated, doing it official.'

Tate rose suddenly. '*In* my office,' he said, 'soon as you're through.' And he went, banging the door loudly behind him. The noise splintered in Hackett's head like a radar jammer swamping the screen with electronic garbage. For a moment Vatan's voice was blotted out by the interference.

Wearily, Hackett said, 'Pardon, M'sieur?'

'I was asking 'ow exactly we can be of 'elp to you, M'sieur.'

'We believe . . . that Jouffret is in contact with an Englishman now living in France. This man is of interest to us. I need to know whether this is so . . . and I need to know it quickly.'

'What is the name of this Englishman?'

'When we knew him,' Hackett said bleakly, 'he called himself Smith, Harry Smith.'

' 'Arry Smith,' Vatan repeated. There was no recognition in his voice. 'And 'ow quickly must you 'ave this information?'

'Before the weekend.' Each time he thought how little time there was, he felt a dull emptiness in his stomach. Vatan gave a soft whistle of surprise. 'He knows,' Hackett thought. 'Not long enough. Not bloody *long* enough!'

Vatan said, 'In that case, M'sieur, of course it would be a pleasure to meet one of our British colleagues who 'appened to be visiting 'ere. We would try to be whatever 'elp we can, which might not be too much since it 'as to be unofficial. But let's wait and see – eh?'

'Thank you, M'sieur,' Hackett said gratefully. 'I

appreciate very much what you're saying. I'm hoping to be with you sometime around the middle of the morning.'

'Until tomorrow then. Au 'voir.'

'Au revoir, M'sieur.'

Hackett put his phone down. He realised he was trembling slightly, nervous reaction combining with fatigue. A lot had been riding on that call. If Commissaire Vatan had decided to play politics he'd not have stood a snow ball's chance in hell of clocking Harry. But now that was the first hurdle over; Tate was the next. As he rose and moved for the door he felt momentarily faint-headed, and knew he was in no fit condition for a fight. He just hoped his boss wasn't as angry as he looked. Half way across the main office he helped himself to a fresh, steaming beaker of coffee on Bonney's desk, and gulped it, scalding, leaving Bonney speechless behind him. At Tate's door he paused, braced himself before knocking, and through the glass saw Tate waiting for him.

They both tried to get a word in first, colliding with each other. 'Good of you to drop by,' Tate said. 'Hope I won't make you late for the plane.' While Hackett was countering with, 'Did mean to tell you, sir, talk it through...'

'Should bloody hope so!'

'Only you were out...'

'Getting my private parts chewed off – all for you, Superintendent! And very painful it was too!'

For a moment Tate glared at Hackett and Hackett looked bleakly back at him, too tired even to try to match the blaze in Tate's eyes. Eventually Tate couldn't stand Hackett's hang-dog expression any longer. 'You look terrible,' he said. 'Better sit down – hadn't you?' Hackett sank gratefully into a chair. 'Now what he hell do you have to go to France for?'

'To find out if Harry Smith is behind this caper in the docks,' Hackett said.

'Harry Smith . . .?'

'The one who used to run Willie.'

'And helped the wife to stitch him,' Tate said, remembering. Hackett nodded. Tate said, 'You think *he's* behind it?'

'Damn sure he is.'

Tate was floundering. 'So what's that got to do with France?'

Hackett slowly collected himself and began at the beginning. He told Tate all about Evie Bellis, and about Harry taking it on his toes to France, and then began listing all the coincidences that couldn't be *just* coincidences. Before he'd finished Tate was ahead of him and knew where Hackett was driving. He acknowledged it as a possibility. But there was something lacking from Tate's voice, and it dawned on Hackett that what was missing was any sense of excitement. Tate was sounding almost bored.

In the end Tate said, 'All right, it's not only possible, it's even probable. But so what?'

Hackett said, 'Sir?' unable to believe he'd heard right.

'Suppose you find out it is Harry. What you going to do about it?'

'Set him up as a target,' Hackett said, stating what was, for him, the blindingly obvious.

'In France?' Something about Tate's tone distinctly worried Hackett.

'Why not?'

'Why the hell do you think he went there in the first place?' Tate asked in exasperation. 'You know why! You told me yourself a few minutes ago!'

Hackett was slow to react. Somehow Tate seemed to be missing the importance of what he was getting at.

Lying low in France or at the North Pole, it didn't matter: it was Harry Smith they were talking about. Harry! Planning a hit on their ground!

'You can run him as a target as long as you like,' Tate continued angrily. 'But you can't lift him, can't feel his collar, can't have him away – not in France!'

'So I'll wait till he comes out,' Hackett said, feeling his own anger starting to rise.

'And if he stays put?! Which, if he's got as much nous as you say, he will!'

'Then I'll winkle him out.'

'How?'

'God knows!' It was very nearly a shout.

There was the briefest of pauses, then Tate exploded. 'What the hell's got into you? You've got yourself obsessed by the man! What good's that? He's like a worm in your brain, Steve! No bloody good to me – that. Not your private war we're fighting. Not some bloody vendetta. Don't you think we've got enough villains in our own back yard? If Harry's in France there's damn all you can do about it. So forget him! And try thinking about a team of hard bastards blasting off sawn-off shotguns in the docks come Saturday!'

When he'd finished there was a short silence. The level of noise coming from the main office had dropped dramatically. Hackett could imagine the grins and knowing glances and fingers being drawn across throats in there. 'Maybe he'll be with 'em,' he persisted doggedly.

'He won't be! But *if* he is – *then* you can have him!'

'Not physically on the job,' Hackett said. 'Harry was never on an actual job in his life. But close: in the country – for the split.'

'Christ!' Tate shouted. 'Don't bloody give up, do you?'

'Only way we could have him would be by proof of association.'

And to get that, as Tate well knew, they'd have to have photos of Harry and Jouffret together – proof of a meeting. Tate rose abruptly, turned his back on Hackett and spent what seemed like a long time just staring at the map on his wall, while he brought his temper back under control. He didn't care for being bearded in his own office, and if Hackett hadn't been such a valuable officer . . .

'I'd still like your permission to go to Bruay, sir,' Hackett said eventually, very wearily.

There was another pause before Tate replied. Without turning, and sounding almost as tired as Hackett, he said, 'I want you back here Thursday morning – at the latest. Now just . . . go home and go to bed.'

He heard Hackett's chair scrape as he rose, but he didn't turn until he'd also heard the door close behind him. Through the glass he watched him slowly weaving his way across the main office. There was an obdurate, driven quality inside him, Tate thought: what made him such a good, hard copper . . . and what would cripple him, in the end; burn him up, burn him out . . . make a God-awful cripple of him – in the end.

Hackett was approaching Bonney and Louise who were standing together at a notice board mounted on the wall. They were looking through a sheaf of photographs of the dead body of Willie Bellis. On the board was a kind of family tree bearing the names of Bellis, Jouffret and Newby with arrows linking them together. Louise indicated one of the photographs and Bonney pinned it on to the board over Willie's name. Shot from above and to one side – the side to which his face was turned – with his mouth gaping stupidly open and strands of hair plastered down over his eyes, there was something almost unbearably lonely and pathetic about Willie in death. The photo covered the arrow leading away from Willie's name. It was the end of all that line. Ahead of Newby and Jouffret lay an open board.

Hackett looked briefly at the photo, then nodded towards his door. 'In, both of you,' he said. They went ahead of him while he paused a moment longer, looking at Willie. He wondered when Harry would know; whether Jouffret would dare tell him. And for some reason, perhaps because once Willie had been the nearest thing Harry had ever had to a friend, and Jouffret would know that, he doubted it. Hard bastard though Jouffret was, Harry was even harder.

Hackett came into the office behind Bonney and Louise and closed the door. 'Jobs', he said, 'for both of you. Bonney, want you to get your backside up to London. I'll sort it with C-11. I want to know who the team is Newby'll be bringing down at the weekend. How many? Who? And what they're good at? So you check his known associates and you watch who he talks to. Right?'

Bonney nodded. 'Right.' At first hearing it sounded fun. It was only when he thought about it afterwards that the miles of dogged, foot-sore tailing, the sitting in pub corners nursing half pints beyond their natural endurance, the waiting and the waiting and the waiting, began to tarnish the prospect for him.

Almost as though reading the thought Hackett said, 'I'll try to persuade C-11 to give you reasonable back-up.'

Bonney grinned weakly. 'Thanks,' he said.

'Louise,' Hackett turned to her. 'You pack yourself an overnight case. We're going on a trip together, just you an' me.'

'Where?' Louise asked impassively.

'Bruay-en-Artois,' Hackett said. 'Which is in France, near . . .'

'Facetious bastard,' she thought, and said, 'I know where it is.'

'Bet you do, too.'

'Staying at the Hôtel Boule d'Or?' she asked, and Hackett nodded. She knew why they were going; had known ever since that moment in the mortuary that he would go; but it had never occurred to her that he'd want to take her with him. In a strange indefinable way she found the idea unpleasant. 'Why me?' she asked vaguely.

Hackett could have said because she spoke the language better than him; or because a man and woman together were good cover; or because he just fancied her company – or her; or even that Bruay in autumn was a place not to be alone in; but he didn't. Instead he said something about – if, for any reason, they needed someone to charm Jouffret he didn't fancy the idea of him having to do it. It was meant as a joke, but Louise obviously didn't find it very funny. It came too close to something she'd felt at the airport the first time she'd seen Jouffret; and, half-submerged in her subconscious as it was, it worried her.

'The morning plane?' she asked. Hackett nodded. 'See you at the airport.' She turned to make for the door.

'So when shall we three meet again?' Bonney asked lightly.

'Thursday afternoon,' Hackett said. 'At the latest.'

After they'd gone Hackett sat a while in dull reverie, feeling the after-effects of his sleepless night tugging him towards a kind of half-conscious stupor. Yet he seemed to lack the will-power to make any move to go home. Besides, there were still things to be done: C-11 to be sorted; plane seats to be reserved . . .

His phone suddenly rang. He felt the first flip of anticipation when he heard it was another call from France. The next came when Vatan said, 'I 'ave some news for you, M'sieur . . .'

That amazing, bloody lovely Frenchman had been at work, checking, already! According to the concierge at the Hôtel Boule d'Or an Englishman had stayed at the hotel three times in the last ten weeks. On each occasion he and Jouffret had spent a lot of time together. The Englishman had registered himself in the name Harold Sloan. And even as Hackett's excited brain was clocking the initials, Vatan was saying. 'But then, one name's as good as any other. Don' we know it, M'sieur?'

6

They took off into brilliant sunshine. It was one of those incandescent autumn days that are like the embers of summer: luxurious with mellow warmth yet softly laden with melancholy. It was this last Louise was most strongly aware of: a slight feeling of vacancy and dislocation, of being adrift, which was partly the way autumn always affected her, and partly the result of this flying into an uncertain future, leaving all her touchstones behind.

And that was odd; because she'd travelled far greater distances than this, into greater unknowns than those which awaited them in Bruay – and she'd done it alone. That last year of her teens she'd crossed thousands of arid miles, mostly on foot or hitching, just occasionally on trains, all the way from Turkey through the Arab States and into India. By the time she'd set off the George Harrison trail had grown cold and the footprints had been blown over by sand; but she'd not been looking for the Maharishi and meditation; she'd just gone to look – at the landscapes and the figures who had skin burnt almost to black, who lived and moved on the landscapes, and were part of them: and in India she'd seen flies crawling over a face of poverty that had been almost unendurable to behold. It had taught her more about life and about herself than London University, from which she'd dropped out to go on the journey, could ever have done.

Yet here, now, despite Hackett's presence, she was feeling strangely apprehensive and vulnerable – lonely even – on this skip-and-a-hop to Bruay-en-Artois for a couple of days' quiet villain-spotting. Stupid, she told herself. All the same, she'd have been glad for some distraction from the thought of what lay ahead, but Hackett was a tactiturn companion: after they'd met at the airport they'd discussed various possible covers, agreed on what seemed the best, then not had much left to say to each other. Now Hackett was reading a newspaper, self-contained and brooding.

Looking out of the window Louise could see fields of yellow stubble patched black behind lines of flame that rippled under drifting smoke; and rich, red acres of newly ploughed earth, hard against the green of fields left fallow, while within the breaks of trees there was a hazy confusion of all these colours coming together. Then, still climbing, the plane banked so that the earth tilted away and all she could see was the sky. When they levelled out again they were much higher, had left the land behind them and were over the sea.

In his paper Hackett read of a youth of seventeen who'd been remanded in custody charged with the murder of a woman twice his age with whom he'd been living. Then, of a combined police operation in which twenty addresses in London and Essex had been raided simultaneously in connection with jewelry thefts, resulting in thirteen people being detained, assisting police with their enquiries. A couple of pages later there was a story about a girl, twenty years old, who'd been raped by some bastard with a knife then forced to drive him nearly sixty miles before they'd been stopped by a police road-block and the man overpowered. Finally he read a report of a trial in which two men had been acquitted of murdering a third because the Prosecution hadn't been able to prove which of them had physically 'done it'! 'Wouldn't like to be the copper who screwed that one up,' Hackett thought. 'God, there's so much of it! Never bloody ending . . . like some guerrilla war that just escalates and escalates...'

If anyone now were to ask Hackett why, at eighteen, he'd joined the police, with benefit of hindsight he'd say – to go to war. It wouldn't be hyperbole. To Hackett that was what it was: a war – in which he'd been in the front line for longer than most wars even lasted. He had the scars to prove it: a broken marriage, sacrificed to war so many years back that if it weren't for the photo of his son he kept by his bed he might have trouble remembering that he'd ever actually been married. But after that bust-up the war had been all he'd had left, and he'd thrown himself into it even harder until it had become like a corrosive love affair in itself: something he needed but which was destroying him with bouts of wildness and occasional flailing despair that were gradually eroding the edge of his professionalism – not that he realised as much, but Tate had glimpsed it and it worried him.

Hackett folded the paper and offered it to Louise. She declined with a shake of the head and he shoved the paper into the seat pocket in front. A hostess was wheeling the drinks trolley up the aisle and Hackett asked Louise if she wanted anything. Again, she declined. When the hostess arrived it was obvious she'd sussed them as a couple who'd be good for business, so when Hackett refused she took it almost as a personal slight. Louise had to stifle a smile and the atmosphere between her and Hackett was better for a while after that.

When the hostess had gone, Hackett said, 'Want to run through it again?'

'What?'

'Our cover.'

'You're the chairman of the education committee of – er . . .'

'Hucknall,' Hackett said.

Louise nodded. 'Which is Bruay's Twin Town. You're in Bruay to liaise with your opposite number about a schools' exchange that's going to happen in the New Year.'

'Good,' Hackett said. 'And what's my name?'

'Steven Hird,' Louise replied without hesitation.

It had occurred to Hackett that if Harry did come to the Boule d'Or, and saw the name Hackett in the hotel register, the whole operation would be blown. So the previous afternoon the passport office had obligingly provided him with a new passport containing the fictitious details of Steven Gregory Hird. Louise was travelling under her own name but with a passport which listed her occupation as 'personal secretary'.

Almost as an afterthought, she said, 'What happens if Jouffret knows that Hucknall *isn't* Bruay's Twin Town?'

Hackett looked almost fondly at her. 'You know what our Twin City is?'

She shook her head, smiling. 'But he might check.'

'Well if he checks,' Hackett replied, 'if he goes that far – then we're already blown.'

The words served as a small reminder that this wasn't just a jaunt they were on, nor was Jouffret just a pudding, and Louise felt that twinge of unease again.

'What about you?' Hackett said.

She hesitated, then with a shrug said, 'I'm the bit of skirt the wife doesn't know about – right?' There was a flatness in her tone, a deadness, that was like the tired acceptance of something inevitable; it was almost the tone of someone who was half-afraid there might be some truth in it.

Hackett caught the inflection and was puzzled by it. He smiled as if she'd been joking and said, 'That what's synonymous with being a secretary?'

She shrugged and looked out of the window at the sea that was grey and green and ribbed with the shadows of the swell. 'Be better,' Hackett continued after a while, 'if you say you think that's one of the reasons I've brought you. You're my secretary, you speak good French, but you think all I really want is to get inside your knickers, and you don't want to play. Gives you an excuse to keep away from me and hook yourself on to whoever else is around. Bit of protection.'

'Jouffret?' she said. 'Protection?'

Hackett grinned. 'Yeah, well let's pretend you're not a very good judge of character either.' She smiled very faintly and looked back to the sea. 'So long as you feel all right about it,' he added.

'Fine,' she said quietly. 'No problem.'

There was a problem, but not one she could admit to him. It was why she had the feeling of vulnerability; it was to do with something in her psychological make-up that she'd tried often enough to rationalise and understand but had never been able to. After all, she wasn't, so far as she knew, a masochist; she had no secret guilt for which she sought atonement through pain; her father-fixation was well under control; and yet with terrifying consistency she seemed only to be attracted to men who were older, probably married, or who had the capacity to hurt her almost beyond bearing. It wasn't something just accidental; subconscious, perhaps, but no accident that again and again she'd found herself forming liaisons that she knew from the start were seeded with pain and destruction. She had no idea why she did it. Occasionally she fought it, but her heart was never enough in the fighting. And that was why she was apprehensive of seeing Jouffret again.

From practically the first moment she'd spotted him at the airport she'd known he was dangerous, and this perverse thing inside her had been attracted by him. Knowing later who he was and what he was, what he'd done and would likely do again, she'd felt sick with herself because, despite the knowing of it, the fascination had remained; still did. And now, here was Hackett pushing her towards him.

'So all right,' she thought dully, 'what the hell? Let's just spin the wheel and play.'

Bruay-en-Artois was a town where it was always Sunday afternoon; and always raining. They'd touched down at Roissy through low cloud into a dull, leaden day with wet hanging in the air. Louise had gone to hire a car while Hackett had phoned Vatan who'd given him directions for Bruay once they'd left the autoroute. Then they'd got into the car, set the wipers going, and headed north.

At first the countryside had all been familiar to Louise. She'd spent a holiday in Senlis not all that many years ago. And yet, as they drove on, through the familiar landscape that passed beyond a haze of drizzle, she'd experienced an odd sensation of familiarity coupled with detachment and vague disappointment, as though watching an old, grainy film of childhood: her memories had seemed more real.

On the autoroute Hackett had driven with his foot pressed to the floor. Conversation had been impossible over the racing of the engine and the roar of juggernauts heading for Belgium or the Channel ports. And steadily the landscape had flattened into a drear sprawl of untidy, monotonous countryside where the trees at the fields' edges were all twisted and lopsided, and where farmers' ploughs still sometimes churned up the odd bayonet or soldier's skull. Occasionally they'd seen the tips and slag heaps and pit-heads of mines; and long, regimented ranks of high-voltage pylons marching north against the sky. Its monotony bore in on Louise, feeding her depression.

They came into Bruay just before one o'clock under a steady downpour of rain. The town was a long, low straggle of dull, red brick and dirty whitewash, with that scrappy, uncared-for air reminiscent of towns in Belgium. The streets were practically deserted. It was the kind of place one would pass through without stopping, and never remember having been there.

On the phone Vatan had said he'd come to Bruay to meet them. There was a park they would pass as they entered, the Stade-Parc Municipal, where he'd be waiting in a white Citroen near the main gates at around twelve-fifteen. By now Hackett expected to find he'd lost patience and gone back to Béthune, but as they drove down the narrow street towards the town centre Louise suddenly pointed. Ahead, through the rain, Hackett saw an arched gateway – and parked just beyond it a white Citroen. He pulled in to stop just in front of it, nose to nose.

There were two men in the Citroen, both in plain clothes. Hackett turned up the collar of his raincoat and reached for his door handle, but then saw that the figure on the passenger side had beaten him to it and was already coming towards them. Louise lent backwards to unlock the rear door. The man dragged it open and scrambled in. He was wearing a raincoat and trilby which, in just the brief distance between the two cars, had become soaked. He was about fifty; a big man with a face that reminded Louise of her parents' old dog: heavily jowled with pronounced bags under his eyes and large ears with thick, heavy lobes. There was nothing delicate or refined about him, though he moved with a sprightliness that was unexpected and the apparent energy of someone much younger. His bulk dominated the confined space of the car. He was smiling, while rivulets of rain trickled down his cheeks.

'M'sieur 'Ackett?' he said, extending one huge hand.

'M'sieur Vatan,' Hackett replied, grasping it. 'I'm sorry we're late.'

'Does not matter,' Vatan said. 'A day like today – all the – er . . . the villains, they all stay at 'ome.'

Hackett grinned and introduced Louise.

'Enchanté, Mam'selle,' Vatan said and kissed her hand. Louise smiled back and felt some of her gloom starting to lift. Vatan was the best thing to have happened all day.

'It's very good of you to meet us,' Hackett said.

Vatan shrugged expansively. 'Think nothin' of it, M'sieur. You 'ave made me curious, that's all. An' when I am curious . . .' He laughed loudly. 'I 'ad 'oped,' he said, 'to be able to guide you to the 'otel, then per'aps talk over a drink or some food. But now . . . unfortunately I do 'ave to be back in Béthune by two; an' by the time you 'ave – er . . . booked in . . .' He shrugged again.

'I'm sorry we're late,' Hackett reiterated. 'I would like to talk . . .'

'Need to talk, M'sieur, of course! But there is no problem. I shall be free later on an' we can 'ave all evening. If that is convenient to you?'

'Perfectly,' Hackett said smiling. 'Shall I come to your office in Béthune?'

Vatan pursed his lips as he considered a moment. 'I think,' he said, 'mebbe you don' wan' to be so far from the 'otel, so far from our friend – eh? So better, mebbe, if I come back to Bruay?'

'Does Jouffret know you?' Hackett asked.

'No, M'sieur . . . but meetin' at the 'otel might be . . .'

'No,' Hackett said. 'Not the hotel.'

'But there is a café,' Vatan said, 'opposite the 'otel . . . Café Franco-Belge. 'Ow would that suit you?'

'Ideal.'

'So we say what? Six? Seven?'

'How about seven?'

'Perfect, M'sieur. An' I 'ope Mam'selle Colbert will be able to join us,' he said beaming at Louise. Louise smiled back.

'If she's not got her hands full by then,' Hackett said.

' 'Ands full?'

Half-jokingly Louise said, 'It's my job to seduce M'sieur Jouffret.'

'Oh – but should 'e get so lucky?' Vatan protested. They laughed, but then his face became quite serious. 'You take care – eh?'

'Of course,' she said quietly, and again she felt the small knot of fear twisting inside her.

Vatan turned to Hackett. 'So – until seven o'clock, M'sieur. Now I 'ave just time to guide you to the 'otel.' He chuckled drily. 'Though it would be – er . . . difficult to miss, you know?'

'It's very good of you,' Hackett said.

Vatan shrugged and started to open his door.

'Is Jouffret at the hotel now?' Louise asked suddenly.

Vatan paused. 'I believe so.'

'And he's not had any visitors?' This from Hackett.

'Not so far as we know.' Vatan smiled again, hesitating; then he said, 'This curiosity of mine, M'sieur, it's – er . . . sometimes 'ard to bear. So tell me what 'e's been up to in England, eh?'

'Planning a robbery,' Hackett said.

Vatan nodded as though that was no surprise. 'It's what 'e knows best,' he said, and climbed out into the rain.

The Hôtel Boule d'Or was quite a large, black and white building looking vaguely mock-Tudor, situated in a street just off the centre of the town. Vatan's car drove past without stopping, just giving a flick of its back lights as Hackett turned in through an archway that led to a courtyard at the rear. The mock-Tudor nonsense stopped as soon as one got through the arch, but it picked up again in earnest as soon as one entered the hotel itself. The reception was heavily panelled, and where the panelling stopped bare, whitewashed brick took over on which phoney, black beams were arranged with meticulous symmetry,

The receptionist offered them a room with a double bed. Louise asked for two rooms with single beds. The receptionist almost visibly shrugged: two rooms they could have, she said, but double beds it would have to be – unless they wanted just one room with two singles: Louise settled for two rooms with a double bed in each.

Hackett lingered over signing the register, letting his eye run down the names on the preceding page, but there was no Sloan or Smith or any other English name. He supposed he hadn't expected there to be, but he couldn't help feeling a slight pang of renewed anxiety. They had just one and a half days in which to clock Harry: thirty-six hours! But what if he didn't come in that time? What if he didn't *need* to come – at all? Maybe Jouffret had made a phone call and that was all that was required. Or he might have gone into Paris before returning here – if Paris was where Harry was. They could have met at a café or on a bench somewhere watching old men in baggy suits and collarless shirts play boules. Perhaps three words were all Jouffret needed to say: 'It's on, 'Arry!' Or . . . what if Hackett was wrong, completely wrong, and it wasn't Harry at all? But that was the unthinkable. It was Harry. He would come. Hackett's obsession demanded it.

Louise hadn't brought much in the way of clothes. She dropped the few bits and pieces into one of the drawers of the dressing-table and rammed it shut. Then she stood still a moment, just letting her glance slowly drift around the room: gold and white striped wallpaper; green and pink striped bedspread – ugh! Reproduction Louis XIV furniture; flower prints mounted in gilt frames, extraordinarily modern light fittings. Had no idea what it was trying to be, she thought; ends up as a tasteless hotchpotch . . . and slightly effeminate. She wondered whether Jouffret's room was similar, and tried to picture him sitting on the edge of a pink and green bedspread looking at frilly net curtains across the window. It was too incongruous. She realised she was smiling to herself.

There was a light knock at her door, and she opened it to admit Hackett. 'All right?' he said, giving her a flick of a nervous smile. She nodded. 'I've seen him. He's downstairs in the bar place.'

'Brasserie,' she corrected him. 'It's called a brasserie.'

'Well he's in there anyway.'

'Jouffret?'

He nodded.

'What's a man like Jouffret,' she said, 'doing . . .'

'In a place like this?' He glanced around and shrugged. The effeminate quality had struck him, too. 'Maybe he's bent,' he said, joking. 'Queer.'

'You better hope not,' she returned evenly, 'or I'm redundant.'

He grinned briefly. He'd wandered to the window and was easing the net aside to look down into the street. It was still raining, hard and incessant. There was no colour anywhere; everything looked grey and gleaming. A few figures scurried along the opposite pavement from doorway to doorway, awning to awning, while the rain danced on the roofs of parked cars and the odd umbrella that came into view. Lights were on in the café and shops across the street. It was so far removed from the day they'd left behind it tended to emphasise their sense of isolation. While they were together the space they occupied was like an island on which they were castaways, forced to make the best of each other.

Hackett let the net fall and came back towards her. She noticed a restlessness in the way he moved, as though he was keyed up with frustration or anticipation and nervous energy. Slumping untidily into a chair he said, 'Order of battle then. Yes?'

She perched on the edge of the bed and said, 'Fine.'

'This afternoon we get the lie of the land. Only I'm going to spend as much time out of sight as I possibly can. Two reasons: I've got a cover to maintain; and I don't want Harry arriving and walking straight into me. So you're the one who stays visible, all right?' She nodded. 'And your main job, so far as you can without getting obvious about it, is to keep tabs on Jouffret.' She nodded again. 'Then this evening, while I talk to Vatan, you close in on Jouffret – if he'll let you.' Her face was a mask of passivity. 'Now: do you want covering while you're with him?'

'I'll be all right,' she said flatly. 'I've done this sort of thing before.'

'If I hadn't known you could do it I wouldn't have

asked you to come,' Hackett retorted. 'All I'm saying is – do you want . . .' He checked himself, then tried a different tack. 'What I mean . . . is that *I'd* feel better if I knew you were covered and had some sort of get-out in case things turned nasty.'

There was a slight hesitation before she nodded casually. He was insisting on her having a lifeline, and she wasn't sure whether she was relieved or angry. Hackett rose and crossed back to the window. After a moment he said, 'From seven onwards Vatan and I'll be in that café.' She wandered across and stood just behind him, looking. 'Get their number, then as long as you stay near a phone you know you can reach me. Idea?'

She nodded once more, almost as though she wasn't much interested.

'And if I'm not there I'll be in my room.'

'Couldn't be safer, could I?' she said lightly, almost mocking him.

He turned from the window and for a moment they were face to face. He didn't know what it was with her but that inflection in her voice puzzled and worried him. It was as though all the time she was trying to put him down. And all he was worried about was her safety. 'That's all right then, isn't it?' he said coolly and brushed past her. At the door he paused. 'Lunch?'

She inclined her head and went calmly to join him.

'Sergeant-major of a Régiment de Chasseurs Parachutistes, you understand?' Vatan said. 'An old soldier.'

'Bloody hell,' Hackett said flatly. 'I've heard about them.'

He and Vatan were at a corner table in the café, which was busy and noisy with teenagers who'd commandeered all the tables down the length of one wall and were shouting to each other, bursting into choruses of laughter and cheering, thumping the tables making the glasses and crockery jump and rattle. Constant in the background was the hiss of the coffee machine. At several of the remaining tables there were small groups of men drinking liqueurs or red wine, playing dominoes or cards. The atmosphere was humid. There was a thin veil of condensation over the windows through which, diffused, they could see the lights of the hotel from across the dark, wet street.

Vatan was drinking anisette while Hackett warmed his hands round a cup of bitter, black coffee. The subject of their conversation was Jouffret. ''Ard men, M'sieur,' Vatan agreed. 'Good in a war. Not so good for us when there are no wars left – eh?' Hackett managed a grim smile. 'On'y they – er . . . they kicked Jouffret out, even before de Gaulle disbanded them. I don' know why. It was a long time ago. After that it's difficult to be sure where 'e was an' when. They think – Algeria; an' after that – south to wherever 'e was useful for 'owever long; an' after that . . . they think – Saigon.' He shrugged hopelessly.

'All the hell-holes he could find,' Hackett said.

'Old soldier runnin' out of wars,' Vatan said again. 'I 'ear now they 'ave the same problem in America. On'y there it's young men who 'ave no use left for the skills Vietnam gave them . . . except to shoot at policemen, mmm?'

'Jouffret . . .' Hackett began, but a roar of clapping and cheering from across the room broke over them. He waited for it to subside. With tolerant good humour Vatan sipped his drink and smiled. Eventually Hackett was able to continue. 'Jouffret,' he repeated, 'here. Why here?'

Vatan shrugged. 'Not where one would expect to find 'im – can be advantageous. 'Undreds of miles from where

’e does ’is business – that’s on’y sensible. ’E moves about, anyway. Never stays in one place too long.’ He shrugged again.

‘Why there?’ Hackett said, nodding towards the hotel.

Vatan smiled. ‘The food’s good. An’ old soldiers like their comforts, don’ they, M’sieur?’

‘Must cost him.’

‘ ’E ’as money,’ Vatan returned mater-of-factly. ‘At Clermont-Ferrand they took over a million francs. At Gap it was four ’undred thousand. It ’as to be damn big for ’im to bother, you know?’

Hackett nodded. For a moment he was lost in his thoughts, seeing Jouffret and Harry together. The more he heard the clearer the picture came. They were worthy of each other. They made one hell of a team.

‘This – er . . . robbery,’ Vatan was saying, ‘that you say Jouffret is planning. Can you tell me about it?’

‘They’re going to hit half a million pounds’ worth of silver bullion,’ Hackett replied evenly. And Vatan gave that soft whistle of surprise again. He was stunned into a moment’s flabbergasted silence, slowly shaking his huge head, staring at the youths across the café but not really seeing them. The row emanating from that side of the room seemed to recede until here it was as though they were in an isolated pocket of static silence, like being in the pool of light from a softly buzzing desk lamp in a dark room.

‘That explains a great deal, M’sieur,’ Vatan said eventually. ‘If I were you, knowing that, I think I would be . . . a very excited, very frightened man.’ He tossed back the remainder of his drink and gestured to Hackett’s cup. Hackett shook his head. Vatan raised his hand and waved a waiter towards them.

When the waiter had gone again Hackett began to relate the whole story, from their first contact with Newby, through to the realisation of what the job was going to be. Vatan listened without interrupting, chuckling occasionally and nodding with pleasure. His new anisette arrived and he raised it to Hackett in a silent toast of admiration as the story continued, moving on to Willie's death and finally Evie's revelation concerning Harry.

When it had all be told Vatan let his digestion work on it for a while. At length he asked quietly, 'You think 'e . . . murdered this – er . . . Willee?'

'Yes,' Hackett said bleakly.

'It wouldn' surprise me,' Vatan nodded. 'At Clermond they killed two people: a bank clerk; an' a woman who just 'appened to be there an' who screamed at the wrong time.' His voice was flat, matter-of-fact. 'My colleagues at Clermont – what they say . . . Jouffret is er . . .' He spread his big hands, hunching his shoulders up. 'Psycho – yes? A psychopath.'

The drink arrived on Louise's table without warning. She half-registered it was a cognac before looking up, slightly startled, although knowing what she'd see: Jouffret. He was smiling. His cold eyes were fixed on her with a kind of lazy intensity. She felt a sudden spurt of adrenalin, a brief flutter of excited satisfaction – that her lure had worked. Her face betrayed nothing.

She'd been in the brasserie for nearly an hour, sitting in a corner beside the huge, blazing fire, facing the bar, sipping a glass or two of St Raphael and immersed in a copy of Harold Robbins's *The Betsy*. Jouffret had been sitting on a stool at the bar drinking whisky. At the most there'd only been about six other people in the bar at any one time. Jouffret had chatted to one or two of them and in a fairly desultory way to the barman, but he'd also spent a lot of time drinking steadily in self-contained, moody silence.

Very, very occasionally, when Louise had glanced up, her eyes had met his. She'd not played the being-embarrassed game, quickly averting her eyes or becoming flustered; that sort of performance didn't sit well on her. She'd simply appraised him, briefly and impassively, then let her gaze drift casually away before returning to her book. After it had happened two or three times she'd allowed herself to give him the faintest of all possible smiles – no more than a brief softening of her features, like a vague acknowledgement of the coincidence; then she'd resumed reading and taken care not to look up again for some time.

It was always a very finely judged thing, this leading on: there'd had to be no hint of encouragement, yet she'd had to implant her presence imperatively in his consciousness. She and Hackett had laid the groundwork over lunch by appearing to have an argument – which hadn't been hard – and which she knew had been noticed by Jouffret. At the end of it she'd walked out on Hackett – nothing loud or histrionic, just a premature, cool departure, which had helped to set up her being alone that evening.

Also in keeping with her cover, twice during the hour she'd been in the brasserie she'd gone out to the public phone in the reception which could be seen from where Jouffret was sitting, and had appeared to make calls that weren't answered. On returning the second time, as she'd passed Jouffret, she'd again allowed their eyes to meet and had given him a cool, polite smile. Settling back to her book she'd thought, 'Now move, you bastard: bloody move!'

The glass of cognac arriving on her table was like a reward.

'Permettez-moi,' Jouffret said.

She hesitated only a fraction then, without smiling,

shook her head. 'Merci non, M'sieur.'

Jouffret ignored the refusal as she'd been sure he would. He lowered himself into the chair opposite her and put his own glass on the table. 'Vous êtes anglaise?' he said. She nodded, remaining perfectly impassive – displaying a hint of irritation if anything. 'I know English,' he said.

'I speak French,' she replied evenly.

'Then we don' 'ave no trouble understandin'.' He smiled again and pushed the cognac further towards her. 'Take it,' he said.

She eyed the brandy for a moment then looked evenly back at him. She didn't want to lose him but the part had to be played. 'I'd prefer St Raphael,' she said.

He regarded her with those hard, lazily penetrating eyes for several seconds. To encourage him, but still cool and without haste, Louise folded down the corner of the page in her book and closed it. Jouffret lent forward, retrieved the brandy and sauntered back towards the bar.

As she waited Louise tried to concentrate her mind on what was to come, but junk and irrelevancies kept getting in the way. The fire was crackling. She could hear the hissing of wet as it steamed from the logs. Someone had put the juke-box on. The record was English: two years old – had to be . . . or longer. It reminded her of something – a dreary surveillance operation in an out-of-season café on a wet promenade, and always the juke-box had been playing this song. Across the bar there was a sudden, loud burst of laughter. She looked at her watch: coming up for eight-thirty. So how long did that give her? Two hours? Three? A noisy party of diners had just entered for pre-dinner drinks, middle-aged business-men and their tarted-up wives whose dresses and hair-dos looked like relics from the sixties. Louise smiled faintly. Then she saw Jouffret heading back towards her, and the junk shunted out of her mind in a rush so that she was amazed how clear-headed she suddenly was.

'Santé,' he said.

She raised her glass in acknowledgement. Close-to like this, in the subdued light with the reflection of the flames catching his face, some of the hardness seemed to be melted out of it. She felt a disturbing sense of unreality. Outside it was a rainy autumn night; in here it was all soft lights and fire-lit warmth. She was on her own, sitting opposite a man she had no difficulty in appraising, to whom she was involuntarily attracted, and who was probably a murderer.

'What's 'appened to your friend?' he said.

'My boss,' she said and shrugged.

' 'Ere for business?'

She shook her head, and casually launched into the lie that was their cover. She did it so well, investing her tone with just the right amount of boredom, that the story was bestowed with total credibility. Jouffret seemed amused by it.

'So what you do,' he said, 'all for kids – eh?'

'What I do,' she returned with an emphasis on the 'I', 'is translate for him, and be where he wants me to be.'

'You don' mind that?'

She shrugged. 'It's a ride.'

Jouffret laughed. 'What they call you?'

'Louise.'

'I don' think you go big on 'im – this boss, eh Louise?'

She smiled coolly. Time to shift the emphasis, she thought, get him talking about himself; and if he wanted to think she positively hated Hackett's guts – well that was fine. She said, 'Your name, M'sieur?'

'Jouffret. Roland . . . Jouffret.'

'Your English is good.'

'Damn right,' he returned. 'Know where I learn?'

She shook her head.

'Saigon.'

She let it appear as if that threw her more than it actually did. Eventually, putting two and two together, she said, 'The Americans?'

'Aussie,' he replied. 'Big fat slob of an Aussie.' He grinned and threw back what was left of his drink. She declined another for herself and waited while he went for more whisky. Saigon, she thought, what had he been doing in Saigon? Pimping? Black marketeering? Running dope to the American boys? . . .

When he came back, although she knew it might be a dangerous area, she said, 'What were you doing in, Saigon?'

'This an' that,' he said bleakly; then, as though privately amused, he added, 'Watch Yanks 'ave good times.' He started on his fresh scotch and she wondered how many he'd already had: not enough to affect him visibly, though his appetite for it seemed to be increasing, his drinking more compulsive and careless. She doubted there was going to be any need for her to have to encourage him. After several swallows he said, 'I been around: Africa – all over.'

'I've been to Spain, Majorca and here,' she lied.

'Bloody pissing-down place, this,' he said, and laughed.

She smiled slightly. 'Ever visited England?' She made it as casual as she knew how, but she was taking a risk.

He looked at her oddly for a moment, and she forced herself to hold his gaze with innocent curiosity in her eyes. Then he nodded. 'I been there.'

'London?'

He shook his head. "Not where you come from.'

'Hucknall? . . .'

' 'Ucknall,' he repeated, and it was like mockery. 'Not been there. Wha's it like?'

'It's another pissing-down place like this,' she said evenly.

Jouffret snorted with laughter. Louise remained impassive, sipping her drink. When he'd recovered Jouffret said, 'Mebbe you give me your address so when I go back . . .' he broke off suddenly.

'To England?' she said. 'Back to England?'

'Finish some business,' he said vaguely and shrugged as though it wasn't important.

Louise felt a mild sense of elation. She knew better than to ask what the business was: stupid to wander any further into the minefield than she need. She could hardly believe how easy it had been. What Jouffret had just told her was that the job was still on. And that, she thought, was about as much as anyone could expect her to get out of him; anything else that came was a bonus. She finished her drink and put down her glass.

' 'Ave another,' he said.

She hesitated, knowing that she must be careful how much she drank, and wondering, also, if there was any point in going on. Safer not to, personally and professionally. But inside her there was a hunger that still wasn't satisfied; and like a treacherous friend to it there came the thought – what else *might* he let slip?

She must have hesitated too long, because he said, 'Unless mebbe you rather we do somethin' else?'

'Oh Christ!' she thought. 'No,' she said, 'I'd enjoy another drink.' He shrugged as though it didn't make much difference to him, and started to rise. 'Only,' she added, 'there's a phone call I have to make. I've been trying to contact someone all evening and I've not been able to get through.'

'For your boss?' There was that edge of mockery in his voice again.

'Yes.'

He just laughed and wandered away towards the bar. In the phone booth she tried to collect herself: she could call Hackett now, get herself out of it, but was that being weak and stupid? Or was having another drink being stupid? What the hell was she *doing* here? She looked at her watch: nearly nine-fifteen. The treacherous friend inside her said, 'Just one last drink: where's the harm in that?' She dialled a random series of numbers; listened to the phone buzz for a moment, then put it back on its rest.

As she returned to the table she saw that the drink Jouffret had bought her was a very large one. For a while they talked trivialities: about the hotel, Bruay, French politics – about which she professed total ignorance, and gathered indirectly from what he said that he hated the socialists and communists – but he wouldn't talk about Algeria or Africa or even Saigon again. He was becoming increasingly reticent, she thought, spending longer just watching her in a way that she found distinctly unnerving. At one point he said, 'We don' 'ave to stay 'ere, if you don' want.'

The clear implication worried her even more. 'I don't mind it here,' she said, wishing that his presence wasn't so dominating and imperious inside her. It was insidious and swamping, dangerously undeniable.

A little later he asked, 'You like drinking with me?'

'Yes . . .' she said awkwardly. 'It's . . . it's very pleasant.' He laughed and took a swallow of his whisky. In an attempt to be professionally constructive and to get the conversation away from the personal, she asked, 'What line of business are you in?'

'What pays best,' he replied, and wouldn't be sidetracked. 'What you like – eh?' he persisted. 'You tell me what you like.'

'In what way?'

'What makes you laugh?'

'I don't know,' she said. 'I think I have an odd sense of humour.'

'What makes you cry?'

'Not much.'

He smiled. 'Cool bitch, aren't you?'

She looked at him sharply, caught off guard. 'I can do without that!'

'Yes?' He took another swallow of his whisky, all the time keeping his eyes fixed on hers.

'Yes! Just buying me a few drinks doesn't give you . . .'

He didn't allow her to finish. Sneering, he asked, 'You sleep with 'im? Your boss?'

For an instant Louise felt stunned, but then, still managing to keep her voice low, she spat back, 'He bloody well wishes I would!' She looked at her book and shoulder bag lying beside her, and wondered why the hell she wasn't on her feet and walking out by now. But this, she realised, without fully understanding, in a way this was what she'd been waiting for: the challenge, the exorcism – and she felt a tangled sense of extraordinary relief and excitement, as well as fear, now that it had come.

Jouffret was chuckling. 'I like that,' he said.

'You can go to hell and back!' she returned with all the contempt she could muster. 'I never asked you to come and buy me drinks!'

'Why don' you walk out?' Jouffret sneered.

'If you don't leave me alone – I will!'

'I think I like to make you cry,' he persisted softly.

'You couldn't do it!' The contempt in her voice was like a challenge.

'You think you're so damn cool,' Jouffret said. 'You come with me an' find out.'

'You've got to be joking!'

'I think . . . you wan' I should make you cry.'

'You're bloody sick!'

'Eh? . . . Why don't you come – eh?'

'For Christ's sake!'

'Make you laugh an' cry – eh? Like you wan' I should.'

'I don't want anything from you,' she said. 'You disgust me!' He was laughing. She could feel it getting harder for her. Christ, he was evil! But his eyes wouldn't leave her alone. The sound of his voice wouldn't stop playing havoc in her head. She should have gone when she still had the will power . . . because he'd read her too well: and he was too bloody good at this!

'You wan' I should make love to you,' he was saying, soft and insidious. 'So come on, you bloody bitch!'

'Christ!' It was like something tearing out of her as she floundered.

'Why don' you say "yes"?'

'It's not true!'

'Why don' you say it louder?'

'I don't want to go to bed with you!'

And he was laughing again. 'Now say it like you mean it – eh?'

She said, 'I don't! . . . Please! . . .' and realised: God in Heaven! She was pleading with him! 'You get some kind of kick out of this?'

'Don' you?'

'No! . . .'

'Lying bitch,' he said, and he was leaning across the table towards her, his face coming towards her; his eyes coming towards her; his hand coming towards her. 'I think you wan' me touchin' your tits . . .' His hand was at her breast in a soft, wicked caress that was like a butterfly on her blouse, and away again as he laughed. The shock of it was like a jolting charge of electricity. On the instant there were tears in her eyes, filling them, blinding her.

The noise in the bar was like the sound of distant waves lapping on a shore she knew now she'd never reach. So this was drowning. She felt a sense, almost, of disbelief that it was actually happening. Through the tears she saw a blurred nonsense of shapes and soft colours. Then, with another shock, only this time duller, she felt Jouffret's fingers stroking the tears off her cheeks with extraordinary, horrible tenderness.

'Now you come with me, eh?' he was saying softly. 'An' I make you laugh an' feel good again. We drink an' we laugh, and we don' cry no more, just you an' me, eh? You come with me an' stop cryin' an' I make you feel so damn good, better than you feel for a long while, eh?'

The mayhem inside her had left her nothing with which to resist. Mechanically she accepted the book and shoulder bag which he pushed into her hands. They rose together from the table. His arm was round her shoulder gently propelling her as they crossed the brasserie. One or two vaguely curious glances followed them, and one or two knowing smiles went like telegraphy down the bar. She passed seeing nothing.

It was only as they came into the reception that the confusion within her had abated enough for her to be aware of one coherent thought: she was blowing it, the whole operation! Even if she didn't care what happened to herself, once she went up those stairs with him she'd blown it; 'technically unprofessional' was the phrase Hackett would use, just before he called her a stupid, bloody cow!

She faltered. 'I must try to make that phone call again,' she said faintly.

He didn't believe she was serious. 'Now?'

She nodded feebly and tried to move away.

'Not now,' he said.

'I must.'

'You don' 'ave to . . .'

'Yes.' Her voice was dead-sounding.

'It's too late . . .'

'I have to try again!' She said it as vehemently as she could. Tears were building once more, and she was feeling more drained than she could ever remember feeling. 'Then I'll come . . . with . . . you!' She jerked herself free and went slowly towards the phone booth. He stayed where she'd left him, in the middle of the reception, contained in hard, cold anger. She shut the door of the booth and leant against the wall, trembling and occasionally still sobbing. She could sense him watching her through the glass. She took the number of the café out of her bag and began to dial.

It seemed an eternity before the phone was answered. There was such a row at the other end she could hardly hear the voice that shouted, ' 'Allô! . . .'

' 'Allô, je veux parler à M'sieur Hird, s'il vous plaît.'

' 'Allô! . . .' the voice said again.

'Je veux parler à M'sieur Hird!' she repeated, louder.

' 'Allô! . . . Pardon? . . .'

'Sweet Jesus!' she thought. She said, 'M'sieur Hird, s'l vous plaît!' and was almost shouting.

The voice said, 'Attendez!'

There was another interminable pause. She had her back to the glass and tried to hold herself steady against the trembling while she shut her eyes and breathed deeply. She didn't dare turn to see where Jouffret was. Suddenly she heard Hackett's voice, saying, 'Hello – Louise? . . .'

'Steve,' she said weakly, tight into the mouthpiece, 'get back here – please.'

The line went dead almost instantly. She hung on for as long as she dare, appearing to talk while the phone buzzed in her ear. Then she replaced the receiver and walked slowly out of the booth. Jouffret was leaning against the reception counter, watching her contemptuously. From there, she thought, there was just a chance he hadn't heard.

'I got through,' she said, with a faint laugh like saying, 'Fancy that!'

' 'Ip-'ip-'ooray,' Jouffret sneered. She took a message pad and pen from the counter and started to write. 'Why you so damned slow?' he said viciously, starting to attack again.

'Please!' she cried, imploring him not to. She signed the message, folded it in half and was reaching for an envelope when she heard Hackett's voice behind them.

'Evening, all.'

She swung sharply, feigning surprise, and trying to keep the relief out of her face and voice. 'Steve!' she said. Jouffret had turned towards him, and the expression on his face had become that hard, closed mask he usually wore. 'I was . . . just going to leave you a message,' Louise said weakly, and with an obvious hint of embarrassment.

'Why?' Hackett said, in what appeared to be deliberate insensitivity. 'Going somewhere?'

She resisted the urge to look at Jouffret. 'Only just to bed,' she replied.

'Bed?' he laughed, obviously determined to wreck whatever real plans she had. 'It's not even ten yet. Come on, I'll buy you a drink.' He strode off into the brasserie.

Louise looked to Jouffret and for a moment their eyes were locked.

'I'll see you sometime,' he said, and it sounded like a promise.

She stood rooted to the spot, trembling slightly, as she watched him going from her, up the stairs and out of sight. She turned and followed Hackett into the brasserie.

7

The way the waitress offered Bonney his breakfast menu was as though to say, 'I know we're supposed to serve breakfast till nine o'clock, but after eight-thirty you're a bloody nuisance!'

He glanced through it in the vain hope there might be something to tempt him. He already felt like something not quite human; after reading it he felt a shade worse: it was imagining all those fried rashers and sausages that did it. He ordered a pot of black coffee, two slices of toast, a glass of water and two alka seltzers. The waitress shot off almost before he'd finished speaking. At several of the abandoned tables around him the breakfast debris was being cleared and places set for lunch. The clash of cutlery as it was shunted on to or off the trays, and the banging and rattling of crockery was a cacophonous insult to his presence: a punishment for his being so inconsiderately late down. He sat in mute misery surrounded by it.

The coffee pot arrived on his table with a jarring thud. At the same moment he saw Clare arrive, coming through the restaurant door. He raised an arm and waved languidly to her. She crossed towards him with a cheerful smile, but one which was edged with tiredness. Her face was pale; the way she moved not as energetic as the day before. It came as a slight relief to him to see that she was suffering the after-effects as well. As she joined him, to the waitress's visible alarm, he indicated the breakfast spread and asked her if she wanted anything.

'Had it,' she said. 'I'll pinch some of your coffee, though.'

He asked the waitress for another cup and saucer. She turned to the next-door table, swiped a clean cup and saucer and banged them down in front of him. That was a punishment as well.

'How d'you feel?' he asked Clare.

'I've felt better.' She gave him a rueful grin. 'How about you?' He shuddered and she laughed.

Clare was the Detective Constable C-11 had assigned to him. She was small, dark-haired, northern in origin, with a bubbling sense of fun and enough innate sexuality to keep anyone's mind off the job. Up until about eleven o'clock the previous night Bonney had entertained certain decidedly ungentlemanly designs on Clare; but Newby had turned out to be a spoil-sport, keeping them on the go until two in the morning, by which time any thoughts of playfulness had been left stranded the wrong side of midnight.

The previous morning Bonney had spent entirely at New Scotland Yard, being guided by Clare through the labyrinth of cross-indexed references to Peter Robert Newby. The team with which he was most closely associated comprised nine men. All but two had form. They went in for banks, security vans, occasionally the odd Post Office. They were a hard bunch who, one day soon, would be stitched for life because C-11 was closing on them. One day soon they'd open up some security van to find it stuffed with policemen; but Bonney doubted it would be in the docks this coming Saturday because these were men who were in business in their own right, not hired help, not even for a share of half a million.

After them the cross-indexing had really come into its own: men Newby drank with; had been seen talking to; had had business dealings with; were members of the same clubs; associates of women he knew; ex-cell mates – anyone with criminal connections with whom Newby had, or could reasonably be expected to have, some form of contact. Bonney had ended up with a list of over thirty names. They'd been able to eliminate a third of those because the men had either died, or were back inside again, or hailed from too far away to be considered serious contenders. Thus, eventually armed with twenty-odd names, a few mug-shots, Clare and Bonney had taken to the streets.

Ostensibly Newby was a car salesman working for a showroom in South Street just off the Chiswick High Road. They'd watched the showroom all afternoon, but Newby hadn't left once, not even to take a prospective buyer on a trial run. If Clare hadn't been such irrepressibly cheerful company, and if Bonney hadn't nursed such delicious expectations of what the night might bring, the boredom would have been almost unbearable. As it was it had seemed almost fun.

When, eventually, Newby had left, they'd followed him to a pub where he'd stopped for a couple of scotches and a hot pie, then on again, heading for Shepherds Bush. In that early evening with the greyness of dusk falling ever quicker, while keeping his eyes fixed on the back lights of Newby's Jag, Bonney had felt a heightened sense of anticipation and excitement. It had been to do with simply being on the move: four days away from a five hundred thousand pound job, and the man who was going to pull it on the move – at last! It had been to do with Clare sitting next to him, and with being in London, off home ground, in traffic that moved faster than he was used to, along roads that were unfamiliar – almost like an adventure. All these elements had come together to make him feel buoyant, light-hearted, so that he'd hummed to himself in pure bloody happiness. And that was the way they'd followed Newby all down the Goldhawk Road into Shepherds Bush Green.

Newby had cut across the bottom of the Green, and accelerated up Wood Lane, past the Television Centre, as though making for the Westway flyover, but then he'd tucked himself in left and his destination had suddenly dawned on Clare.

'He's coming to the dogs,' she'd said.

And been proved right. In the floodlit White City Stadium they'd merged into the roaring crowd to watch greyhounds streaking round the track: and between the shifting, bobbing dance of heads to watch Peter Robert Newby join three other men at the trackside, and talk.

To the untrained eye nothing could have looked more innocent or casual: but to Clare and Bonney it had been obvious that the four men were more interested in what they had to talk about than in the dogs that flashed past them. And Clare had been able to put names to two of them: Roger James Stott, CRO of sixty-four, convictions for robbery and demanding with menaces; and Terence Croft, CRO of the same year, convinctions for theft of motors and GBH. The third man, younger than the others, she hadn't known.

Scott and Croft were both freelancers, up for hire. Croft had a reputation as a wheel man; Stott was just brute strength. They came in on jobs for a fixed fee, did what they were paid to do and went away again. As the nucleus of a team for Saturday's job Bonney reckoned they were dead right. Watching them through the crush of spectators, as they'd talked, laughed, occasionally following the burst of dogs from the traps, with the roar of the crowd going up all around them, he'd felt a sense, almost, of personal achievement with everything going his way.

Coming up for nine-thirty Newby, Stott and the third man had left together. They'd piled into Newby's Jag and headed up West. And that was when the evening had started to deteriorate. One pub had followed another, right through closing time and out the other side. There'd been no more contacts; just steady drinking, and playing of juke-boxes and fruit machines and pinball tables. Despite his designs on Clare, however, Bonney had been reluctant to quit, because however promising a start Croft and Stott were, he'd known there had to be more. He wasn't sure how much half a million in silver bullion actually weighed, but he was damn sure it was more than five men could handle with any speed: only four when you discounted the driver.

And that was the quandary still facing him as he'd come down to breakfast the next morning. Newby and Co had made a night of it. The pub-crawl had been followed by a vast Chinese meal in Soho; and still no further contacts had been made. Bonney's sense of achievement had become submerged beneath mounting perplexity. The evening had started so well, his expectations had been so high, but by the time he'd collapsed into bed, alone, just after three in the morning, he'd felt only a confused sense of disappointment and frustration, as though the whole affair had somehow tilted towards disaster.

Across the breakfast table, over the rim of her coffee cup, Clare's eyes managed a rueful twinkle. 'A whole new day,' she said. 'Exciting, isn't it?'

Bonney grinned weakly. For him, this new day had only one question to answer: who and where were the rest of the team?

It was perhaps unfortunate that he never seriously considered the possibility of there being no others – that he'd already seen the whole team: because if he had, it might have occurred to him either that Newby's calculations had gone awry, or that there was some kind of mistake in someone's thinking . . . somewhere.

Louise wasn't in the dining room when Hackett arrived down for breakfast. She wasn't in her room when he tried ringing half an hour later. From the receptionist he learned that she'd gone out early on. With his imperfect French and the receptionist's non-existent English he had a worrying moment when he thought the girl was saying that Louise had actually booked out, but eventually he gathered that she'd simply taken an early breakfast, then gone out.

Outside the hard rain had stopped, but everything was still heavy with wet, the air laden with a drizzle so fine one couldn't actually see it. The greyness remained dominant. Above, and for as far as one could see, the sky was a flat, low wash of cloud. A car, swerving suddenly in to the kerb, splattered Hackett's shoes and trousers with black water. Disconsolately he meandered around the small town centre which could almost have been the centre of any small mining town in the north of England even, hard and brash and faintly depressing. He caught no sight of Louise. He wasn't sure he was specifically looking for her. The thought of staying inside his room at the hotel had been enough, on its own, to bring him out.

Almost without realising it he was leaving the centre behind, his steps taking him out on the road by which they'd entered Bruay the previous day. In places the pavements were littered with grit and small stones, washed from the gap-tooth patches of scraggy land between the dreary rows of houses. Coming up beside the park there were wet leaves choking the gutters. He turned in through the arched gateway, and mounted a shallow flight of steps to come on to a broad path between bedraggled flowerbeds, sullen beeches and dripping firs. There was the smell of wet earth, and rain on leaves, and that faint tang of wet, mouldering decay. The path was completely covered in a slippery patchwork of leaves and blasted petals. He strolled on for several yards but, feeling his footing to be unsure on the wet surface, had almost decided to go back . . . when he saw Louise.

He might have known this would be where he'd find her. She was sitting on a wrought-iron bench at a bend in the path, turned away from him, looking over grass bound in by poplars and shrubbery. She glanced up as he sat down beside her.

She was relaxed and very still, but placidly so: like a pastel figure in a wet landscape. He didn't know how to begin; so they sat watching the heavy drops fall from the leaves, while the drizzle that was too fine to see softly blurred the distances like mist. And after a while Louise took the burden away from him.

'Is it possible to forget about something?' she asked quietly. 'Utterly and completely?'

'No,' he said, knowing to what she was referring. 'Once something's been experienced it's known and lasts for ever.'

She seemed to accept that, although he suspected it wasn't the answer she'd been hoping for. She was quiet for a moment, then she said, 'Possible to put it out of one's mind then, for most – if not all – of the time?'

He thought for a moment, then nodded. A touch bleakly he said, 'Hope that's good enough for you.'

Very simply, she said, 'I'm sorry. I'm better now.'

Hackett rose. 'Come on,' he said. 'Harry'll have been and gone by now. Let's go back to work.'

Harry hadn't even been, let alone gone again. Louise brought the news to Hackett in the Café Franco-Belge opposite the hotel. She noticed the way he involuntarily glanced at his watch, as though time was beginning to run out.

Which it was. Tate had said that he wanted them back by Thursday morning – at the latest. Effectively it meant their returning that evening. The one direct flight from Roissy took off at six, and to make that the very latest they could afford to leave Bruay would be four. It was after eleven now. 'Less than five hours,' Hackett thought. 'Christ, why doesn't he come?'

'We could catch a later flight to Heathrow, get a car there and drive home,' Louise suggested.

The idea was like a reprieve to Hackett. Louise went to phone Roissy for flight times through the night. She came back to announce that there were three, the latest an Air France departure at twenty-one twenty hours, which would give them until seven. 'Eight hours in all,' Hackett thought. 'He's *got* to come!'

They were prisoners now, of time and events, chained to the hotel and the café opposite. Waiting was never easy, though at times their job seemed to entail nothing else: waiting in hope. But it was never easy, and as the day drained west it became a kind of torture. It affected Hackett more than Louise, though she was caught up in it: there'd been too great an emotional investment in this jaunt, one way and another, for it to be wasted now. She was apprehensive of what might happen if the climax never came: apprehensive of what it might do for Hackett.

They packed their bits and pieces and vacated their rooms, leaving their cases in the car. After a snack lunch in the café Hackett remained there while Louise went back to the hotel and ensconced herself in the residents' lounge from where she could watch the reception desk. She opened her Harold Robbins but quickly found reading virtually impossible.

She caught sight of Jouffret just once, as he handed his key in to the desk, on his way off somewhere. She was thankful that he didn't see her, though relieved to find that the sight of him affected her hardly at all.

Apart from the occasional guest who wandered in and then out again, she had the lounge to herself for the whole afternoon. Several men booked in during the time she was there, but only two were on their own and neither even remotely fitted Hackett's description of Harry. She looked at her watch and was shocked to see it was nearly six o'clock. She felt her emotional balance give a lurch; hope starting to sink, to be replaced by a dull sense of despondency. It was getting too late: the odds against anything happening now . . .

In the café Hackett tried to prepare himself, psychologically, for failure. Intellectually it was easy: of course he'd been gambling, asking too much, expecting too much, relying on luck, chasing shadows . . . and all the rest of it! Now he had to reconcile himself to the fact that Harry wouldn't come: that he'd probably never know whether he'd been right or wrong; that possibly his last chance to nail Harry Smith was almost gone. And that was where the intellectual exercise floundered; because as long as there were seconds left to run, his mind refused to let go of that tatty banner of hope he carried like some Don Quixote in rusty armour. What was it Tate had said? 'He's like a worm in your brain, Steve. Don't you think we've got enough villains in our own back yard?' Well he was right and he was wrong: Harry *was* the worm in Hackett's brain, the wound and the puss and the cancer: but none of the villains in their own back yard quite measured up to him. Harry was a walking offence to nature.

Without Harry, Hackett thought, what did he have? He had Jouffret, Newby, others whom Bonney should be clocking now. He had a plan to lift half a million all set for the docks this coming Saturday – only he'd be there and he'd lift them, which was better than nothing. At least this trip had confirmed that the job was still on. So what he had was better than nothing. But it wasn't enough!

He saw the café door open and Louise enter. For a moment she was like a gust of air come to stir his tatty banner. But then he saw her face and knew she had nothing for him.

Unhappily she said, 'I think it's time, isn't it?'

He refused to look at his watch.

'Steve . . .' she urged gently.

'You go,' he said.

She shook her head. 'Saturday in the docks: it's a big operation. Yours. There's a lot of planning to do.'

He knew she was right which was why he resented it all the more. But she *was* right. He rose abruptly and went to the bar to settle his bill. She waited for him by the door. As he joined her she could see the bleak anger in his face. He was moving with brutal speed. It was going to be as bad as she'd feared.

As they crossed the road he said, 'Promised I'd phone Vatan before we left.'

'We're cutting it very fine,' was all she replied.

In the hotel reception he shut the door of the phone booth with a bang that made the glass rattle. He took out his diary, found Vatan's number and dialled. After a moment the ringing was answered. 'Commissaire Vatan, s'il vous plaît,' he said brusquely.

'Qui êtes-vous?' the voice said.

'Hackett.'

'Attendez, M'sieur.'

He waited. He leant against the wall of the booth and glanced back out into the reception. Louise was standing near to the desk, watching a guest register. It was a man. It was Harry Smith.

Hackett literally almost dropped the phone. He was momentarily transfixed with shock. Harry Smith. There was no doubt about it: six years older, carrying more weight than Hackett remembered, but still holding his cigarette between the third and fourth fingers of his left hand – exactly as Hackett remembered; still that slightly puckish face which women like Evie Bellis found so appealing. It was Harry.

Hackett struggled to pull himself together. He turned abruptly so that his back was to the glass. Over the phone he could hear Vatan's voice saying, ' 'Allo, M'sieur . . . 'Allo . . .'

'M'sieur,' Hackett said quietly, 'he's here. Now. Right outside this booth.'

'Who is?'

'Harry Smith.'

There was an appreciable pause from the other end, then Vatan said in a tone of dry humour, 'Congratulations, M'sieur.'

Hackett's grin was like a nervous reflex. He was shaking very slightly, having to make an effort to keep his voice calm. 'I don't think he's clocked me.'

'Seen you?'

'No . . .'

There was a rap on the glass behind him that shot his nerves to ribbons. As he jerked round the door was being opened. He came face to face with Louise. Harry had disappeared.

'Be quick!' she said.

'Name?' he asked desperately. 'What name?'

'Sloan!'

Into the phone he said, 'He's using the name Harold Sloan again.'

'Booked in just for tonight,' Louise added quickly.

'Only staying one night,' Hackett relayed to Vatan. 'M'sieur, I'm aware it's a lot to ask of you, but is there any way the Police Judiciaire could find out where he's living?'

'For you, M'sieur,' Vatan said, 'I'll see what we can do. I'll phone you at your office. Now you should go.'

'Thank you, M'sieur. I am most grateful.'

'Mebbe you do the same for me one day,' Vatan said and laughed. 'My compliments to Mam'selle Colbert. Au 'voir.'

'Au revoir.'

Hackett put down the receiver and looked out of the booth. Louise had gone to stand by the stairs. She gave him an almost imperceptible nod. Trying not to appear in too much of a hurry he crossed to join her, and together they made their way out through the rear exit into the car park.

It wasn't until they were in the car that the mental merry-go-round they were riding began to slow and allow them to think clearly. It had happened so quickly and unexpectedly they were still trembling and felt spent, as though they'd had to run like sprinters to catch themselves up.

'This was where he came from,' Louise said, 'just after you'd gone into the booth. I knew it was him. I was afraid you'd not see him in time.'

Hackett grunted an apology of a laugh. He was leaning across her, fumbling something from the dashboard pocket. She saw it was the camera and knew what he had in mind.

With a hint of alarm, she said, 'The plane . . .'

'Sod the plane!' he returned angrily. 'You've got to see Harry and Jouffret together. You've got to be able to stand up in court and say they know each other. And a photograph of them talking would make it a hell of a lot easier. Only – for Christ's sake . . .'

'I know,' she said. The slightest hint that Harry and Jouffret were being watched, let alone photographed, would blow the operation wide open. With almost fatalistic resignation Louise stuffed the camera into her shoulder bag and climbed out of the car.

She was gone for over twenty minutes. To Hackett it seemed like hours. He sat in a state of almost total inertia, still feeling numbed with the shock and the relief of it; not quite able to believe it had happened. But then, in the moments when it was real for him, it was his obsession haemorrhaging in his brain. He'd been right: it was Harry; it *was* Harry . . . he'd been dead bloody, bang-on right! Harry Smith! Last of all that bad team – back at it! Only Hackett was going to have him!

As the minutes dragged and Louise still didn't reappear an ache of fear began to grow. She was good: but Harry was the most acutely surveillance-conscious man Hackett had ever come across. The tiniest occurrence out of the ordinary would be enough to make him slap on the stops, and the thought of that happening now brought a light sweat to Hackett's face. He wished he'd not given Louise the camera: it was enough for her just to see them together, for God's sake! 'Come on, Louise,' he thought, 'where are you? . . .'

She came out of the hotel looking as cool and contained as ever. She crossed to the car with a firm, calm step. 'I had to wait until they went into the dining room,' she said as she climbed in. 'They're having dinner together.'

'See you?'

She shook her head.

'Did you get . . . ?'

She nodded calmly and took the camera out of her bag.

'Unjust bastard,' Hackett thought of himself. 'Course she did.'

He started the car and put it into gear. 'Well done,' he said, conscious that such spare praise did little justice to what he was feeling. 'Been a hell of a two days.'

She looked at him evenly a moment, wondering what was in his thoughts. 'Got what you wanted, anyway,' she said.

'Yeah,' he said grimly. 'And some.' He grinned at her, feeling a sudden sense of release, like a sun-burst of happiness that made it a pleasure to tease her.

'You've got one hour forty to make that plane,' she replied evenly, and looked away. But he saw that very faintly she was smiling.

8

Bonney woke on the first alarm: he'd set two, one timed to go off ten minutes after the other; but he came out of his light, dream-ridden sleep so instantly that the back-up was redundant. He groped in the darkness to switch it off, then lay, slowly collecting himself.

Saturday. Today. The caper in the dock. Whatever was going to happen would happen today. That was why he'd set the alarms so early. He felt a twist of nervous excitement in his stomach. For a moment he listened, but there was no sound in the house, or in the street outside his window: it was as though it were still the middle of the night. It wasn't – quite: but it was early enough. The darkness in his room was profound, with not even a suggestion of grey by which to distinguish the edges of his curtain.

It was musky and warm in bed. He'd pulled his clothes up to his nose and was breathing the warm air. The disinclination to move – into the cold and hazard of the day – was almost like temptation. He denied it to himself, but still he didn't stir. It was so easy just to lie here, while what was waiting out there was all unknown bar one sure element – there'd be danger. Before the day was out, all too appallingly easily, someone could be dead: an innocent passer-by caught by a ricochet; or a policeman, riddled and ripped by the hot blast of a shotgun . . . One of his friends? Him?

'Give over,' he told himself contemptuously. 'It's time to go to work.'

He switched on his lamp and swung his legs out of the bed, then felt the cold air hit him. Shivering in spasms he sat on the edge of the mattress, his teeth chattering. The coldness seemed to have got inside him already, but that was the chill of fear: he'd have that with him all day, or at least until the action started; then, with luck, he'd not have time to be afraid. Until then, it was something he had to contend with the best he could. At least it wasn't a new sensation; and he'd learnt the best way of dealing with it was, as far as possible, to keep on the move. It was a similar feeling – albeit more acute – to the one he always experienced before a bike race. He dealt with both situations in the same way, steadily getting ready, not rushing things and not dawdling either, so that there was always something to go on to, always the next stage to be borne in mind. It wasn't a bad thing to be frightened anyway, before a caper or a race. What mattered was staying in control, pacing the rate of nervousness, so that the sharpness of one's reactions and one's adrenalin flow were peaking just as one went into the start. That way, depending on which it was – a scramble or an operation – one stood a chance of winning the race, or of coming out of the caper more or less in one piece.

Bonney was pleased with the way he contended with fear: he'd almost made a science of it. It helped, too, to treat it as something entirely run of the mill, although if he'd ever allowed himself to think in detail about the reality of some flak-happy maniac loosing off a shotgun at close range, probably he'd have found his legs gone to jelly and last night's dinner all over the floor.

Still shivering he padded out to the bathroom and splashed water on his face. Looking in the mirror he saw that one of his eyes was slightly bloodshot. His beard needed trimming. He took a pair of nail scissors from the cupboard under the mirror and snipped off several of the worst-offending straggles of hair, but then he decided it was too cold to stand around, and anyway – what the hell? – today it didn't matter what his beard was like.

Back in his bedroom he started to dress, choosing gear that was warm and substantial. The weather forecast for their area had been 'cold and wet'. 'Bloody English climate,' he thought. 'It was lovely only a few days ago.' He pulled a heavy-duty sweater over his head. On top of his jeans he dragged up thick, black leather bike breeches, which felt like diving gear and creaked as he moved. Then he began the business of strapping on his boots.

It had almost the qualities of ritual, this garbing in leather, like a black knight arming for battle. The red in the chequered scarf which he now tied loosely around his neck was the only other colour he wore; like a girl's favour, only too sporty by far. Psychologically the strapping on of leather certainly equated, subconsciously, with the strapping on of armour. It gave him a feeling of completeness and protection, not only against the weather but also against the worst of whatever the day might offer.

His shivering had stopped now. He was still cold inside, but he felt taut and primed. He picked up his gloves and black leather jacket, which he slung over his shoulders, glanced one last time around the room before switching off the light, then went out and along the passage towards the kitchen.

He put the kettle on for coffee and decided there was just enough milk for him to have a bowl of cereal as well. He knew he ought to eat a proper breakfast because God only knew when he might see his next meal, but his stomach was too tight and uncertain; cornflakes were as much as it would accept. The clumsy noises he made as he moved seemed deafening in the stillness, as though they couldn't fail to wake the others in the house. In an effort to be quieter he found he was holding his breath, but even when he exhaled again the silence all around remained almost tangible.

As he sat drinking his coffee he began to feel ready to think about the operation again. When he'd told Hackett that he'd only been able to clock three other members of the team his boss hadn't seemed unduly perturbed, so he'd not let it worry him any more either. The *Swan Royal* was due to be alongside 'P' Wharf by ten hundred hours; the silver should all be ashore by ten thirty. Depending on which route it followed the security van took between seventeen and twenty-eight minutes to get from the dockside to the vaults in the city – but that was academic. Given the amount of time Jouffret, Newby and Bellis had spent in the docks themselves it was almost a certainty that the hit was going to take place somewhere between 'P' Wharf and Jamaica Street. The previous morning Hackett, Louise and he had gone over the ground, and they'd spotted the obvious place. The road ran across a broad sweep of railway tracks between lines of stationary trucks. It was hidden from the sheds and Port Authority offices by the bulk of grain silos, windowless and sparsely manned. The security van was bound to slow as it crossed the railway lines; the wagons gave enough cover for an army to lie in wait; *and*, the nearest dock gate to that point was the only one not bedevilled by a level crossing. So that, they'd agreed, was where it would happen, and this morning would be the centre of their operational web.

He finished his coffee and dumped his mug and bowl on the draining-board. It was still deathly quiet. Glancing at his watch he saw that it was nearly five. He yawned and stretched, and was conscious of a residue of tiredness still lying cold and heavy inside him. 'Keep moving,' he thought. 'Time to go.' He picked up his leather jacket from the back of a chair and shrugged it on, forcing his balled fists through the elastic wind baffles at the cuffs. Then he loosely folded his scarf at his throat, tugged up the zipper on the jacket and pulled the belt tight through the buckle. Picking up his gloves, he glanced around the kitchen then unlocked the back door, switched off the light and went out.

The darkness was intense, bitter, heavy with silent drizzle that stung his cheeks as he came into the wind. It seemed impossible that the dawn was less than an hour away. Even wrapped warm and strapped in as he was, he flinched slightly and shuddered at the misery of the weather. He went striding down the garden as quickly as his leather would allow, finding his way easily in the familiarity of habit. At the bottom he unlocked the door of the shed and stepped into the smell of oil and petrol and stale exhaust fumes. This was where he housed his racer. Flicking on the light, which was momentarily blinding, he glanced at the frame of the scrambler hanging by pulleys from the roof. Its engine was in small pieces laid on oily dust-sheets spread over the floor and workbench. The sight brought a brief, rueful smile. The bike had been in that state for too long now. Somehow, since he'd been promoted, there'd seemed no time any more to get down to putting it all together again.

He turned away to the brute of the BMW sitting on its rest by the wall. His helmet, with its boom-mike attached, was lying on the seat. He put it on, arranged his scarf in a loose fold over the mike, then drew on his gloves. Taking the weight of the machine against his body he eased it off its rest and wheeled it to the door, paused to switch off the light, then went on out, shutting and locking the door behind him.

The wind was still full of drizzle as he pushed the bike through the garden gate into the rough lane at the back. 'What a sodding, miserable, bloody start,' he thought. He swung himself astride the seat and pulled down his visor. Ignition on, petrol on, gear out: he stood on the kick-start and rammed down. The engine caught first time. He opened the throttle to let it rip for a second, blasting the darkness, then he switched on his lights and engaged gear, felt his back wheel skid in the mud and the bike lurch sideways; then the wheel found its grip, the bike kicked away, and he was off, roaring into the darkness.

The factory was about five miles from the scene of the operation, situated in a quiet, run-down street off the main coast road. It was in the heart of the old industrial wasteland which had been superseded by more modern estates when the new docks had been built further down the estuary. The factory was a brick monstrosity. In the grey, tedious dawn light a few tatty 'For Sale or To Let' boards could be seen tenuously adhering to the walls below lines of filthy windows which were covered with rusty, wire-mesh grills. A high brick wall surrounded the yard which was all cobbled sets and vast, muddy puddles, through which the arriving cars churned in steady procession.

As Bonney swung in through the dilapidated gates he saw that between twenty and thirty vehicles were already there. Most were unmarked cars, though there were a few red and white Traffic Division Triumphs and Jags, which he guessed would belong to the backstop teams who'd be manning the roadblocks on the perimeter, maybe eight miles back from the front line. There were a few Crime Cars, Docks Police vehicles, a couple of Transits, two dog vans, a small coach, one or two other motorbikes . . . and behind him, yet more cars following him in.

He left his bike in the lee of a wall and joined the grey, sleepy straggle of men making for the double doors leading into the factory. The arrival of more cars and the splashing of their wheels through the puddles created a constant backdrop to the sound of the men's footsteps on the cobbles, the odd low voice, the quiet chuckle. But there was no real animation, just as there was no real colour in this grey, early light: too early for most of them; too cold; their bodies moving mechanically while their minds shied away from what lay ahead, or were bored by it, especially if they weren't front-line troops. For some it was just another bloody caper.

Inside the cavernous shell of the building, moving listlessly under the harsh, flat glare of floodlights mounted above the windows, and on the iron girders that carried the roof, there already looked to be over sixty people: mostly men, just a few women. Nearly all the men were in plain clothes: reefer jackets, donkey jackets and jeans, anoraks, men in baggy trousers wearing old suit jackets that didn't match, over layers of sweaters and shirts; the odd grubby raincoat . . . clothes to make them inconspicuous around a dock at nine in the morning. Among them there were pockets of uniformed officers: the Traffic men, Docks Police, dog handlers . . . and others: the ones who were to be armed, the so-called police marksmen, six or seven of them, a sober little group, keeping much to themselves and away from everyone else. All but two were to be in the back of the van, armed with Smith & Wesson '38s. The two were to be stationed on top of grain silos with Parker Hale rifles: they were the lucky ones, out of range of shotgun blast; they were also the ones the others worried about, because if they had to fire, and weren't as good as they were cracked up to be, Christ only knew who might get hit; or where a ricochet might find its home!

For this operation Hackett had specifically chosen marksmen from the City's uniformed branches since they'd all be out of sight until Newby and Jouffret had made their move, by which time it wouldn't matter; and if all the policemen who had guns were in uniform, there was less chance of their shooting each other by mistake. It was a point on which he was somewhat sensitive: there was a door in the City in which, still embedded three years after the event, was one of his bullets. It had missed a Detective Sergeant from another Division by a matter of inches, and that only because Hackett had been firing from eighteen or so yards when Smith & Wessons are only truly accurate up to ten. In the heat of the moment he'd been under the appalling misapprehension that the Detective Sergeant was one of the villains. It had been a salutary lesson.

People were still arriving, the total number swelling towards the nineties. Even so, the level of noise in the echoing space was lower than one might have expected. True, there was a general buzz of conversation, even isolated pockets of laughter, but the hour and the weather and what the day had in store combined to dampen excessive conviviality.

At one end of the factory floor a makeshift platform of trestles and planks had been erected, on which there were two chairs, a blackboard with its face presently covered with brown paper, and a projector screen. Tom Cubbon was now setting up a slide projector in front of the platform, opposite the screen. Standing a short distance away, watching, Bonney saw Louise and Dukes. Grinning amiably he ambled towards them.

'Don't be too cheerful,' Louise said as he arrived. 'Please.'

'Feeling fresh as a daisy, me,' he lied.

'Fresh as a daisy that was picked three days ago,' Dukes said wearily.

Bonney grinned and was still trying to think of some riposte when Louise touched his arm. He turned, and saw Hackett and Tate making their way down the room towards them.

Not all the noise died immediately: not everyone had seen them: not everyone present even knew who they were. But the message seemed to get around because by the time they were clambering on to the platform, conversation had dropped to a murmur and there was an air of stiff, tired anticipation; dutiful rather than enthusiastic.

Hackett himself had only achieved five hours sleep. Anticipation, impatience, excitement and fear had churned inside him through half the night. He wasn't the sort of General who slept well on the eve of the fray. The intervening hours seemed such dead time, like an insufferable barrier between him and the climax of hope and planning and expectation which had been building, in this case, with accelerating tempo throughout the past week. Now, looking back, it seemed only yesterday that Newby had arrived for the first time from London: yet emotionally it seemed a lifetime ago. This was how his life lurched, from climax to climax, each approaching peak bought at the expense of frustration and nervous energy, and a gambling with hope that was like emotional Russian roulette.

In all honesty this caper had been straightforward enough, the pieces all falling his way, luck on his side: but he had more invested in this caper than most. Riding to the sound of the trumpets this day was his obsession with Harry: like a grinning skull at his shoulder.

Taking his stand on the platform, however, he managed to present at least an outwardly calm appearance. It was his job, now, to give these ninety-odd people the boost they needed, jaded and twitchy as they were, to go out and do what had to be done and do it well. Gazing over them, his troops, he thought what a lot there seemed to be. But in reality he knew that there were only just enough. Once the tactical groups had each gone their way – the backstop men out beyond the City, the Docks Police to man their gates, the contingency patrols out to cover the route from the docks to the vaults in case they'd got it wrong and the hit wasn't planned to happen inside the dock at all – once they'd all split up they'd be bloody thin on the ground, as usual. But they were enough, just enough, because they *had* to be.

He turned to Tate. 'You want to kick off, sir?'

Tate grinned and shook his head. 'They don't want to hear me. Just lending you the weight of my presence, that's all.' He sat on one of the chairs, crossed his legs and leant back. Hackett turned to face the troops again, moving slowly to the centre of the platform. 'Lights,

Tom!' he called. At the back of the room Cubbon switched off all but the farthest two floods so that they were suddenly in grey gloom. The mutter of conversation slowly died until there was an almost unnerving silence, into which the odd, nervous cough dropped like distant, muted airgun reports on a still day.

Hackett cleared his throat. 'Information,' he said, and paused for effect. 'A week ago, Peter Robert Newby,' a surveillance photograph of Newby clicked up on the screen, 'who is a low-grade member of a team of armed robbers working out of Chiswick, came up from London to meet with Roland Jouffret.' Cubbon shunted the slide projector across and one of the photos Dukes had taken at the airport appeared on the screen. 'Jouffret is a Corsican, known by the Police Judiciaire to have committed armed robberies in France; and with William Archer Bellis . . .' the slide projector clicked and one of the photos taken in the hotel bar appeared. 'Willie Bellis: then, ten days out of prison after having served six years of a nine-year sentence for armed robbery. Willie Bellis has since died, or been murdered; not our concern today. But from surveillance, and in the absence of information to confirm this – I say again: in the absence of precise information to confirm this – our best judgment is that Newby, Jouffret, with others, intend to attack the delivery of a cargo of silver bullion – ingots of silver worth half a million pounds – from the ship *Swan Royal* which will berth at 'P' Wharf this morning – in a little under three hours from now.'

There was no reaction from the troops. So it was another counter-robbery job: so it was half a million quid's worth of silver: so what? It was all known, known and experienced in some form before; routine. Passively they listened in a kind of twitchy boredom.

'Intention,' Hackett said, and again paused for effect.

He knew they'd heard briefings like this often enough before. But it all had to be said; and there was a theatricality to the way he did it that was geared to instil in them some sense of urgency, keying them to the kick-off. 'My intention is to arrest Newby, Jouffret and the others they bring with them, in such circumstances that they may be charged with conspiring together to commit robbery.'

'And before they blow anyone's bloody head off,' Tate interjected quietly. Hackett managed a bleak smile, but no one really laughed out loud.

'Lights, Tom,' Hackett called, and Cubbon switched on the floodlights again, making people blink and shuffle in the sudden harsh glare.

'Method,' Hackett said and moved to the blackboard which he now uncovered to reveal a large aerial photograph of the docks. 'We shall have a Command Post set up here.' He pointed to the roof of one of the grain silos. 'It will be manned by Detective Chief Superintendent Tate and Detective Sergeant Johnson. The *Swan Royal* will lock in from the sea and berth alongside "P" Wharf – here. The route that will be taken by the security van carrying the silver from the ship to the vaults is marked in red. It is our expectation that they'll hit us in the docks themselves, and if I were them, the place I'd choose would be here.' He indicated the area of the freight sidings. 'But it could be anywhere on that red line, any time, once the van starts to move.'

'I will be in that van; and with me will be five men, armed: Constables Bennett, Drake, Esmond . . .' As each man's name was called he raised his arm to be recognised by the rest. Casually curious glances dwelt on them. So they were the ones who'd be carrying shooters. In a police force where still, despite the increasing frequency of its necessity, the carrying of firearms is generally disliked, these marksmen were viewed with a mixture of emotions: idle curiosity, that in some was tinged with awe, and in others with cynical amusement . . . until it was remembered that if shooting did start, these were the men most likely to get shot. '. . . Kavanagh, and Sergeant Mortimer. Two men with rifles, Sergeant Tunstill and Constable Godfrey, will be stationed here . . . and here.' Hackett's finger jabbed to two more of the grain silos overlooking the freight sidings. 'Now: snatch teams – that's Detective Sergeant Cranmer, and Detective Sergeant McLeod – ' the two men raised their arms ' – will be here inside "B" Shed, and here on the outer perimeter road. The word we've been hit will be . . . *Diver* – and the snatch teams will move in on my word: *Diver* – Go, Go. Clear?'

Cranmer and McLeod both acknowledged.

'We'll be on the ground and staked out an hour before the bullion comes off the ship; so you get on the ground – fast and quiet. Radio check then radio silence. Clear?'

This time there was a more general, mumbled acknowledgment.

'One last thing,' Hackett said. 'Among these bastards there *may* be a man called Smith: Harry Smith. And if he is . . .' Hackett turned to look at Tate and seemed almost to be addressing him alone. 'I want him. He's mine.' Tate smiled and gave a small shrug. Hackett turned back to the others. 'Questions?'

McLeod raised his arm and called, 'How many of them are we expecting there to be, sir? Top weight?'

'We don't know,' Hackett replied. 'We can more or less count on five. How many do you want?'

There was a ripple of laughter through the troops. McLeod grinned. 'Five's just fine,' he said and turned back to his team.

There appeared to be no more questions. Hackett

turned to Tate. 'Sir?'

Tate rose almost lazily and came to the front of the platform. A slight buzz of conversation had already broken out, and a shuffling of men impatient to be on the move. The noise died again. Tate surveyed them for a moment. He said, 'Good luck,' and that was all. He nodded to Hackett and stepped down from the platform. The briefing was over.

Men surged forward to look more closely at the route on the photograph. Others turned for the doors. The lofty space of the factory was suddenly filled with noise. Tiredness was being put behind them: the day was that much older; the operation that much nearer; it was time to change gear.

Turning away from the photo on the blackboard Bonney passed Hackett who gave him a small, edgy grin. 'Got a twitch on – have you?'

'There is nothing, sir,' Bonney replied cheerfully, 'us ordinary, unassuming heroes cannot do!'

'Yeah, well you just take care, y'hear? Don't go skinning your arse. It's not so much you we're worried about. Just don't want you bending our bike.'

Bonney laughed and sauntered away towards the doors. As he came out into the yard the noise of the starting and gunning of car engines broke over him, ripping the still quiet morning, one after another; then came the creaking of springs and suspensions bouncing over cobbles, and the splash of wheels surging through puddles as a steady procession of cars rolled out of the yard, through the constant drizzle that was like a veil over the day. At the same time, turning in through the gates, there came an unmarked Transit. It was only when he saw the wire mesh-reinforced windows that Bonney realised it was the Security Company's bullion van. He watched it park close to the factory doors. A man in the firm's livery climbed out of the cab and went staggering into the building carrying several spare sets of uniform and three visored helmets.

Given a choice, Bonney thought, between riding his bike and riding trapped in that tin can, he knew where he'd rather be. He didn't envy Hackett or the marksmen. He tried to imagine what it might be like, five men cooped in the windowless back of the van, on the move, waiting for it to happen. Chances were, the first they'd know would be when some bloody truck half rammed them off the road. He shuddered slightly. He kicked his bike into life and went weaving away, around the puddles, like he was on some obstacle course, feeling gratefully free.

In the factory Sergeant Mortimer and his team were strapping flak-jackets on over their tunics – all except Kavanagh and Bennett who were fastening the flak-jackets over their shirts. They were the ones who, like Hackett, would be on view, wearing security company uniform. The flak-jackets were heavy, bulky carbon-fibre jobs that you sweated under and made fast movement almost impossible: sufficiently so for there to be a valid argument that they were as much a liability as protection. But on a close quarters job like this Hacket had insisted that they be worn, though he'd declined one for himself.

'Any special orders, sir?' Mortimer said. 'About when we fire and when we don't.'

Hackett didn't reply for a moment. It was the greyest area of the whole business. Not on to tell a copper to wait until his face had been shot away before firing back. But anything else left one defenceless against error of judgment: a split-second decision that might result in tragedy, like some poor bastard half a mile away getting chopped by a ricochet from a shot some copper should never have fired! Where was the middle ground? The sure way? There wasn't any.

Eventually he said, 'If you believe beyond a shadow of a doubt that they are going to fire, at you, or at anyone else, you shoot. And to kill, if you have to.' It made him feel weary for a moment, the unresolvability of it.

'Mr Tomlin, Steve,' Tate said behind him.

He turned and found himself facing the uniformed figure of the Managing Director of the Security Firm. 'Morning, Mr Tomlin,' he said and shook hands. 'I understand you're going to drive for us.'

'Rather it was me than one of the men,' Tomlin replied.

Hackett nodded. 'I'd like you to put a flak-jacket on, if you don't mind.'

Tomlin thought about it for a moment. The implications came singing clear. 'I see,' he said. 'I'd rather not, you know?'

'Afraid Superintendent Hackett is going to insist, though, aren't you, Steve?' Tate said gently.

'That's right, sir,' Hackett said. He knew what Tate was thinking. If, today, it happened that Tomlin should end up dead, when the Coroner asked Hackett how come, at least he could say, 'I insisted he wore a flak-jacket. There was nothing more I could do.' It was sensible and it was practical, and what the hell was wrong with covering yourself as well as protecting the man? Logically – nothing. But it made him feel shabby and uncomfortable, because he couldn't be sure he wasn't more interested in covering himself than in protecting the man. That was certainly where the balance of Tate's interest lay.

'Hope the uniforms fit,' Tomlin said, gesturing to the spare outfits he'd laid on the platform. Hackett nodded, smiled bleakly, gestured to Kavanagh and Bennett, and they went to change.

Five miles away, on top of a grain silo inside the dock and overlooking the freight sidings, Detective Sergeant

Johnson finished rigging a dipole aerial, stringing the wire to a radio transceiver similar to the one in the Squad's Intelligence Bureau. A folding table was erected next to the transceiver, and a couple of chairs. The drizzle softly settled on them like grey dust. The detective slid a pair of binoculars out of their case and casually trained them on a point at the furthest extremity of the docks, just before one found the grey water of the estuary. A black and red funnel came into view, seemingly so close that it hit his eyes with a jolt. He swept the glasses for'ard and found the Gulf America house flag, blue and gold, on the foremast. It was the *Swan Royal*, still coming through the lock, the bulk of her obscured behind sheds and tank farms and vessels already in the dock. Before the glasses misted over in the wet, cold air, Johnson decided that the ship had moved, looked as though it was almost through the lock now, so he turned to the table on which lay the operational log. It was a foolscap-sized book of ordinary lined pages. Below the entry which read 'First sighting *Swan Royal*' he now wrote, '08.42 hours: *Swan Royal* through lock'.

The transceiver beside him suddenly crackled static, then a man's voice came through. 'Base, this is Flour Mill, d'you read?'

He leant across to the transceiver microphone. 'Read you, Flour Mill.'

'On watch,' Flour Mill said. And Johnson thought, 'Here we go: it's starting.'

They came on to the dock in dribs and drabs, some on foot, some in cars, undistinguished men slouching through the grey, wet morning, quickly absorbed by the seemingly haphazard bustle of the place. They made their radio checks, then loitered like malingerers, or men having a quick, crafty smoke, in the doorways of sheds and empty port-a-cabins, around parked artics, or watching yellow forklifts dodge in and out of stacks of tea-chests and crates of oranges. They sat in cars parked inconspicuously among others on scrappy stretches of rank grass and gravel; and they smoked and did crosswords, or drank coffee from flasks, hemmed in by the rain, hearing the terse, sporadic exchange of radio checks. And they waited, in a nervous lethargy of anticipation, for what the next few hours would bring.

In the factory yard Hackett, wearing his security guard's uniform and holding his visored helmet under his arm, checked his team into the back of the bullion van. They went clambering in like paras into the belly of a transport plane on their way to the big drop. They were tight and contained, flicks of nervous humour coming off them like static – 'I get travel sick in the back of vans . . .' Sergeant Mortimer was the last in, with a nod to Hackett and an involuntary lick of his tongue over dry lips. Hackett swung the doors on them, and heard Mortimer slam the locks over.

A last few cars were pulling out of the yard. Cubbon was locking the factory doors. He gave Hackett a brief wave as he headed away. Hackett took a last look round and bar the one or two cars that were staying here, could see little sign that they'd been. The next time they'd be there would be for the debriefing when it was all over.

'When it's all over,' Hackett thought. He glanced at his watch and saw that it was just gone nine-thirty. Time to start rolling. Bracing himself with a slight tightening of his muscles against the fluttering in his stomach he climbed into the cab beside Tomlin.

'How'd you feel, sir?' he asked.

'Bit shaky,' Tomlin admitted.

'You've not been hit very often.'

'No. No, the record's not bad. Bound to happen though, I suppose.'

Hackett nodded blankly. As long as there were men like Harry it was bound to happen: and there'd be men like Hackett trying to stop it. He dumped his helmet in his lap and slid shut his door.

'Time to go, I think,' he said, nuzzling his cheek against the skull at his shoulder.

In his office in Jamaica Street, Latimer, the Gulf America agent was on the phone to the Port Authority building inside the dock. 'Is the *Swan Royal* alongside yet?' he asked.

The girl told him it would be about another thirty minutes. Latimer put down the phone and for a moment debated whether it wouldn't be worthwhile to go and pay off the crews of *Swan Castle* and *Swan Hunter*, which were already in, then come back for the wages for *Swan Royal*. But he didn't want to have to make the journey twice so, since no one had started screaming for their money yet, and being a practical sort of chap, he decided he'd stick to his usual procedure and pay off all three crews in one journey, as soon as *Swan Royal* was berthed.

He remembered that today was the day the police expected the silver to be stolen. But that wasn't until it was off the ship and in the hands of the security company: not his concern. He stood at his window and sipped a cup of coffee, watching the drizzle silently seek out all the nooks and crannies of the street.

9

It was Louise who saw them first: Newby, Jouffret and

another man sitting in a Cortina parked in Jamaica Street. She looked just long enough to be sure, then turned her head away and said tersely to Dukes, 'Turn right!' He looked at her in surprise, then realised with a jolt, from the expression on her face, that they were in business. Once round the corner Louise raised her microphone. 'Sir – Louise...'

'Louise – go,' Tate said, from the Command Post.

Our friends are with us – say again: they're with us. Jamaica Street. Waiting, looks like. They're in a blue, Mark Three Cortina.'

'Roger, Louise,' Tate responded. 'How many on board?'

'Three. Jouffret, Newby and another man.'

'Steve – y'read?'

'Roger,' she heard Hackett reply. 'Must be more somewhere.'

Louise looked to Dukes. 'Let's stay clear of Jamaica Street from now on.'

'Why? Reckon they know you?'

'One of them does,' she said quietly.

From the top of the grain silo, through his binoculars Tate followed the progress of the security van as it crawled between shed towards the distant wharf at which the *Swan Royal* was now berthed. Ranging ahead of the van he could see dock cranes already at work, hoisting cargo nets bulging with sacks of fish-meal up from the for'ard hold and down on to the dockside. There, yellow forklifts were hauling the trailers into which the nets were landed back to the central section of the wharf where the sacks were being unloaded and stacked.

Tate swung his glasses back across the dock and minutely began to cover the ground behind the truck. There was no sign of the Cortina. Among the lines of stationary freight wagons nothing moved. It didn't perturb him yet. There was time.

While Johnson stayed scanning the ground he crossed to the transceiver mike and briefly alerted all units as to the security van's position, and that there was no further sign of their friends. Then he paced in a slow, tight circle, feeling his trouser legs grow heavy with wet. 'Not long,' he thought. They could reckon it in minutes now: minutes away. He thought how extraordinary it was that everything down there could be this quiet, this excruciatingly normal, when they were only minutes from being hit.

'They're approaching the ship,' Johnson said.

As they turned onto the wharf Hackett experienced a mild sense of déjà-vu. He was able, for a moment, to see again very clearly the small, drab, huddle of figures clustered around Willie's body, the way they'd been as he and Latimer had driven up. Incredible that it had only been a week ago. It seemed now like something in his distant past, totally divorced from his being here today.

But it only lasted a moment, because the scene which now confronted them was so different. The hull of the *Swan Royal* towered above them as they came into its lee. Forklift trucks droned past swerving and jerking towards the trailers of cargo in little starts and feints, vying with each other to get in first. There were maybe a dozen bedraggled dockers on foot, unhitching the nets from the crane hooks as the loads settled with astonishing precision into the trailers, and rehitching empty nets to be winched back down the hold. It was a smooth, immaculate operation; the timing just right, the trailers in just the right positions, the crane drivers hitting their mark again and again without the slightest hesitation. You could tell the men were professionals, Hackett thought, by the way they made it look so easy.

Tomlin drove past this flurry of activity and pulled in about three-quarters down the length of the vessel, close to the afterdeck. He turned the van and reversed it towards the wharf's edge so that no dockers or prying eyes would be able to see into the back once the doors were opened.

'Go and clear us with the First Officer,' he said, and clambered out. Hackett slid open his door and emerged into the clinging wet. He stood a moment, ostensibly putting on his helmet, in reality scanning the stretch of wharf and the gangs of dockers further aft, looking for anything that wasn't quite right. There was nothing: no blue Cortina, no suspiciously idle hands, no one paying the van any undue attention. He strolled round to the back and thumped on the doors. Almost immediately they were opened and Kavanagh and Bennett, both in company uniforms, climbed out, helmets on, visors down. Sergeant Mortimer and the other two constables remained hidden inside.

'All right in there?' Hackett asked.

Bennett nodded almost curtly.

'Yeah, well relax,' Hackett said softly. 'There's nothing going to happen here.'

It was futile advice. Even he couldn't follow it. They paced, describing listless circles like dogs on tethers, getting steadily wetter, waiting and watching, looking ahead. Hackett was thinking about Harry, wondering if this one time he'd break his rule and *be* there. Maybe this time was big enough, special enough . . . besides, what was he going to do about the split? Even if they had a bullion dealer already lined up, Hackett thought, in this country, would Harry trust Jouffret to take back his share of half a million? Half a million! How big a slice of that was for Harry? Even after a bent dealer had devalued it because it was hot and difficult to handle, they'd still walk away with over three hundred grand. 'Christ,' Hackett thought, 'take a hundred grand off the top and call that Harry's – surely he'd not trust Jouffret to carry all *that*?'

Tomlin came striding down the nearest gangplank and rejoined him. 'They've almost finished cutting through the doors,' he announced. 'Should only be five or six minutes now.'

From inside the shelter of an open-ended trailer shed Bonney, still sitting astride his BMW, looked out over a broad swathe of freight lines, scraggy undulating land clad in nettles and sorrel, and a deserted stretch of dock road that ran parallel to the Basin, but was sandwiched between the grain elevators and railway. A mile and a half, straight ahead, was the Jamaica Street gate; half a mile in the other direction was the one gate not obstructed by a level crossing. It was between here and there, if they were right, that the hit was going to happen. From this vantage point Bonney reckoned he should be able to see anyone heading up through the dock for the freight sidings. So far nothing had moved.

From time to time over his radio he heard Tate asking whether anyone had visual contact yet. Judging from the lack of response no one had, and Bonney understood the mounting tension in Tate's voice. They were leaving it a bit bloody late! Suddenly Hackett was speaking, 'Bullion starting to come ashore now.'

'Roger, Steve,' Tate said. 'Be advised, they're here: but we don't know where yet.'

'Bloody marvellous,' Hackett returned sourly.

He'd got a twitch on himself, Bonney thought, grinning. You could hear it . . .

The sound of a vehicle approaching from behind suddenly cut through his thoughts. He twisted, and saw a red pick-up truck obliquely framed in the far opening of the shed. There were two men in the cab. It passed out of view as it came along by the wall. It was going the wrong way to be of interest, but Bonney vaguely wondered what it was doing on this backwater of a road. Taking a short cut through the docks? It came into sight again, swinging round his end of the building, and for a brief moment he had a clear view of the two men. They were both in overalls. The shock as he realised that he knew them was almost like a physical punch: the driver was Roger James Stott, his passenger the younger man Clare had been unable to identify. They were past before the realisation was fully upon him. He felt suddenly hot with apprehension, wondering whether they'd also clocked him, and for a while that got in the way of the second realisation, which finally came like an echo of surprise: they were heading in the wrong direction!

He pressed his transmit button and began to call urgently, 'Sir – Bonney: Bonney to Base, y'read?'

'Bonney – go,' Tate said.

'They've got a truck, red pick-up, gone by me, Back Dock Road, heading East.'

'Clock 'em?'

'Yeah – Stott, somebody Stott, an' a fella we don't know . . .'

'Roger, Bonney.'

'Say again,' he said vehemently, 'they're heading away from you!'

'Heading where?'

'East, towards Jamaica Street . . .'

'Christ,' he heard Tate mutter. 'Bastards are gonna hit us off the dock . . .'

Bonney rammed down his kick-start and hurled out of the shed, ignoring the bend in the road and ploughing straight over the rough scrub beside the railway. He'd lost sight of the truck. It had turned right, he'd seen it turn right, back towards the Basin: and that didn't make sense either, not unless the stupid bastards had got themselves lost, and surely to God that wasn't possible? So stuff the rest, Bonney thought, he was going to find that truck!

In his office Latimer finished counting the bundles of banknotes into a cash delivery bag and snapped it shut. He was carrying nearly forty thousand pounds; wages for three crews back from three long hauls, with overtime and bonuses thrown in. He didn't often carry that much money; maybe only twice a year when two or more Gulf America vessels were in on the same tide. It didn't unduly worry him. The total journey was less than a mile. And who was to know what he was carrying?

Willie Bellis had known.

Latimer came out of the Gulf America office on to the raised pavement. He walked a few yards to a gap in the ornate railing, and dropped down steps to his Fiat parked below. He chucked the cash bag on to the seat beside him, and started the car.

Thirty yards behind him Newby and Jouffret, with Croft at the wheel, watched the Fiat from their blue Cortina. As Latimer nosed out against the oncoming stream of traffic Newby nudged Croft. Latimer took advantage of a gap and pulled away.

'Go,' Jouffret said.

Hackett watched Kavanagh and Bennett hump the last bullion box into the back of the van. He gave them a nod and they climbed in after it. The doors were banged shut and the locks secured.

He hoisted himself into the cab beside Tomlin, who said, 'Now it starts – eh?'

Hackett gave him a weak grin and picked up the microphone. 'Sir.'

'Go, Steve.'

'Rolling,' Hackett said, and the van began to move.

Radio traffic started to increase now, Tate checking that all units were reading the van, and Hackett maintaining a terse commentary on their progress. On top of the grain silos Sergeant Tunstill and Constable Godfrey settled themselves more comfortably against the parapets, nursing the butts of their Parker Hale rifles into their shoulders, as they scanned the ground through the telescopic sights. Out on the perimeter road, and within the gloom of 'B' Shed, the snatch squads held themselves taut, engines running, waiting for the word. Inside the back of the bullion van the five policemen unclipped their holsters, and felt the yawning emptiness of fear in their stomachs, the taste of sickness in their mouths. Every jolt over the rough road was like the first instant of being rammed. The van rattled like tin cans on a windy line, set to scare off birds: the noise was such they had difficulty in hearing the approach of other cars. They were trapped inside noise and steel, unable to see or hear what was happening outside, feeling their nerves stretch towards the limit of endurance as the seconds passed.

They were off the dock now, accelerating down a long straight past low, red-brick buildings and clusters of port-a-cabins, rank patches of wasteland, the endless backs of cargo sheds. There were artics and trucks, vans and cars, and as they approached each one Hackett was conscious of bracing himself, instinctively, against the sudden blur of movement, the cutting across their path, or the crunching sideways slam as they were hit. Over the radio Tate was saying that they still had no visual contact, and a level of worry that lay only just below panic was starting to rise in Hackett's mind.

They came over the freight lines at a clattering crawl, targeted in the hard focus of binoculars and telescopic sights trained from the silos at their back. 'Here,' Hackett thought, 'it should be here!' They jolted between the lines of wagons and came out the other side unscathed. Hackett thought, 'Where the bloody hell *are* they?!!'

Over the railway the van swung right towards the Port Authority buildings, and the last intersection before coming into the busy main thoroughfare leading to the Jamaica Street gate. A Fiat passed them, travelling in the opposite direction. Hackett thought he vaguely recognised Latimer, but before he was sure his attention was diverted by another car some distance behind the Fiat: it was a blue Cortina, containing two . . . no – three men.

'Got 'em!' He exclaimed. Tomlin's face jerked towards him, suddenly drawn and white 'Coming up now!' Hackett called into the mike. 'Ahead of us, coming on . . .' He slammed down the visor of his helmet, not to be recognised. The Cortina came steadily on. Hackett was conscious that Tomlin was slowing.

'Keep going!' he said, and braced himself.

The Cortina was near enough for him to see Newby's face quite clearly now. There was just enough time for him to feel a pang of disappointment – that the driver *wasn't* Harry – before the bullion van and the Cortina passed one another . . . and in utter disbelief he realised that nothing had happened: nothing had happened; that he was still braced hard against a danger that was passed – gone . . .

'That blue car,' he said to Tomlin. 'Where?'

Tomlin didn't understand what was happening. Bewildered he looked in his outside mirror. 'Going away from us . . .'

'They've passed us,' Hackett said tersely into the mike. 'They've just gone straight past us!'

There was a brief, ominous pause before Tate came back to them. 'So why didn't they hit you?' he said.

Latimer was never really aware of the Cortina behind him. He wasn't aware, either, of the red pick-up truck that suddenly emerged from concealment among ranks of container trailers, and tagged on behind. At least, he wasn't aware until it was all too late.

He'd turned between two sheds taking a short cut towards the Basin when the Cortina started to overtake. He eased off his accelerator to let it get ahead. As it pulled away he became aware of the pick-up truck looming in his mirror, also trying to overtake: it was crowding him, too close . . . and then things happened with such speed that he only knew, with that awful, helpless sense of disbelief, that he was into an accident.

Inexplicably the blue car in front of him suddenly slewed broadside on right in his path. He slammed on his brakes. He thought maybe he'd skidded, because there was a sudden jolt and crunch of metal as his car was kicked sideways by the overtaking truck. It flung him against his seatbelt. The crunch became a grinding noise, metal buckling and glass shattering, and with a flash of bewilderment he realised he was still being rammed sideways by the truck, then the wall of the shed hit him. It flung him the other way making his head crack against the window: and in the haze of pain that followed he dimly perceived figures lunging towards him from the blue car. It wasn't for another second, not until he registered the black balaclava helmets pulled over their faces, that he finally came to understand what was happening. And almost instinctively he grabbed for the cash bag, as though he could actually protect it, even against the sawn-off shotgun he saw one of them brandishing . . .

Jouffret and Newby out of the Cortina, Stott and the

younger man out of the truck swinging pick-axe handles, they came in a vicious rush on the Fiat. Jouffret stood directly in front of the car, levelled the shotgun by his waist and fired. Latimer hurled himself sideways as the windscreen disintegrated where his face had been.

Newby screamed at Jouffret, 'No!' Jouffret started to reload. Stott was dragging open Latimer's door. Newby went ducking in, grabbing for the bag. He managed to get hold of it and hauled, but whether Latimer's grip was vice-like through fear or determination, the agent wouldn't let go.

Newby grabbed a handful of Latimer's hair and dragged him over by it, half dragging him out of the car, while Stott and the younger man smashed their pick-axe handles over the agent's back and arms. Latimer was crying in pain. Having got his head hanging out of the car Newby swung the door and slammed it on his face. The pain was like fire erupting in the agent's head. He couldn't see for a mist of blood boiling at his eyes; couldn't breathe for the blood and smashed teeth that were choking him. He let go of the bag.

Two sheds away Bonney had heard the bark of the shotgun. Others might have mistaken it for a backfire. He'd known it for what it was. Booting the BMW down through the gears he came roaring round the sheds, and through them, hurtling in one side and out the other, kicking the beast round corners so tight, his mastery over the machine seemed near to magic. The blasting roar of the engine, the squeal of the tyres, his skill at harnessing all that brute power, gave him pleasure that was almost ecstasy. And hurling into the narrow road between sheds F and G he saw the red pick-up: he saw Latimer's Fiat crumpled against the wall: and men running...

'They've hit! They've hit!' he yelled into his mike. 'Between F and G sheds! . . . F and G sheds! Looks like a hit! !'

While he was still shouting he was changing down again – and charging: a black knight into battle.

Newby, Jouffret and the others were running for the Cortina as they heard Bonney's bike.

'Come *on*!' Newby yelled.

Stott and the younger man hurled themselves into the car through the open back door. Croft was revving the engine. Clutching the cash bag Newby scrambled to get the passenger door open, then he saw that Jouffret had stopped and was standing his ground, waiting for the motorcyclist.

'Come *on*!' Newby yelled again, like a scream.

Jouffret brought the shotgun up to his waist and waited.

'You bloody maniac!' Newby screamed.

And mad Jouffret swung towards him, loose and easy and too bloody fast, never even seemed to aim the gun – at that range didn't need to – and the blast plastered little soggy bits of Peter Robert Newby all over the car. Jouffret was swinging back again before what was left of Newby had hit the ground. And Bonney was charging on, on, on . . . and Jouffret fired the second barrel.

Bonney met the blast at twenty yards. He was already sliding the bike diagonally across the road. He felt the shot hit him like hail, only harder, slamming him; lead plucking at his leather, shredding it; a stinging and burning in him like hot needles; and the impact of it kicking him back off his seat so that he'd lost the bike. In the same instant that he knew he really was shot, he knew he was coming off his charger.

He was still travelling at nearly forty miles an hour as he hit the road. One foot had somehow got caught in the machine. The bike crashed on top of him, and he was screaming in multiple agony as they slithered together, man and bike, the last few yards across the road; then his head smashed against the wall of a shed, and his consciousness exploded into darkness.

Jouffret wrenched the cash bag out of Newby's dead hand and started to climb into the car. The three men within were looking at him in numb disbelief. Already there was the sound of police sirens wailing towards them.

'Let's go!' Jouffret said.

Stott and Croft reacted almost simultaneously. No way . . . was that madman going with them! Stott rammed his pick-axe handle into Jouffret's side, forcing him back out of the car. Croft let in the clutch. The car kicked forward. Jouffret, half-in, half-out, and only just beginning to realise what they were doing to him, felt his legs go as the car moved. He screamed, 'No! . . .' and clung on with the door banging his body and his feet and legs dragging on the road as they squealed into the corner round the end of the shed. The impetus flung Jouffret away, still holding the shotgun and the cashbag.

The younger man shouted, 'The money! . . .'

'Piss the money!' Croft yelled back. There were flashing blue lights in his mirror and the sound of sirens coming from every direction.

Dragging himself to his knees in the road Jouffret screamed, 'Bastards!' And that's how he was, on his knees, in the wet, ramming fresh cartridges into the shotgun, as the first police car came upon him. As the driver hit his brakes he wrenched the wheel over, drifting the tail of the car into the kneeling figure with the gun. Jouffret went sprawling; and before he had time to lift himself up again there were policemen all over him.

Croft was as good with four wheels as Bonney was with

two, but he was a stranger there, didn't know his way about or where the dead-ends were. And against so many police cars, pouring in apparently from nowhere, he never really stood a chance. Eventually, facing yet another dead-end at an open lock gate, he simply stopped the car and the three men put their hands up.

Hackett stood bleakly watching as two ambulance men lifted Bonney on a stretcher into the back of the ambulance to join Latimer. They were both alive; neither was critical, although Latimer's face wouldn't ever be quite the same again, and Bonney had a leg broken in at least two places, as well as a peppering of lead shot to be extracted. His leathers, like armour, had saved him from the worst of it, plus the fact that it was only the edge of the blast that had actually caught him.

'Lucky,' Hackett thought. 'God, were they lucky! Them and me both.'

He was still feeling off-balance and shaky. The enormity of his mistake appalled him: a whole operation based on a wrong assumption from beginning to end. Not half a million: forty thousand; not silver bullion: cash; not a security van: just one defenceless little bloke in his little motor. Hackett closed his eyes as he thought of it. It was all his – the whole balls-up. He smarted under it as though it was a con Harry had pulled on purpose. Harry! What was Harry doing sending the likes of Jouffret after forty thousand? It was modest even by the standards of six years ago. Not much of a come-back, Hackett thought: not exactly blazing back into the big time! The contradiction of his expectations with the reality of what had happened left him numb with bewilderment.

He walked a few yards towards an untidy heap in the road. As he came nearer his stomach turned over.

Newby's chest and face were a pulp of shredded, bloody flesh. One the concrete blood was spreading in the soft rain, mingling with oil in psychadelic puddles.

There were footsteps at his back 'We've got them,' Tate said.

Hackett turned slowly, heavily, and nodded. He was embarrassed to meet his boss's eyes. There was a leaden pause.

'There'll be questions about this, Steve,' Tate growled quietly.

Hackett nodded again: and couldn't stand the stench of death at his feet any longer. He walked away towards the watching policemen.

The questions came sooner than Hackett or even Tate had expected. The Assistant Chief Constable (Operations) postponed his press conference especially to hold a preliminary post mortem. He wasn't a malicious man, but Hackett had never greatly inspired his confidence. Always there'd seemed something too wayward, too unruly, about the way Superintendent Hackett conducted himself; and now he'd been responsible for what could only be called a carve-up; an abortion of an operation. He'd had over ninety policemen on the ground, and every single man-jack of them had been looking the wrong way when the villains hit! So the ACC wasn't going to wait two weeks for the papers on the job to reach him; things needed to be said now!

Unfortunately for him, in Tate's view, there were more important things to be done the morning after an operation, especially as this was a redundant exercise, one that would have to be repeated in an official form once all the papers had been submitted and read. It inclined Tate to be more protective of Hackett than normal, thus rendering the wicket the ACC had chosen to bat on somewhat bumpy.

'Mayhem, Mr Hackett,' the ACC said quietly. 'Bloody shambles.'

'Yes, sir,' Hackett agreed tersely.

The ACC shuffled the papers on his desk for a while, then got up and went to his window, looking out over the park stripped bare by autumn winds. Tate and Hackett waited. Eventually Tate said, 'We did get them.'

'No thanks to Mr Hackett,' the ACC said. 'We've got a bloody maniac blasting off his shotgun all over the auction, and where are our marksmen? Cooped up in the back of a bloody van two miles away!'

'The bullion was the logical target,' Hackett said.

'So you put all your eggs in that one basket?' the ACC returned contemptuously.

'We were on the right ground at the right time – and we took them!' Tate said again.

'More by luck than judgment,' the ACC retorted 'One man dead. Two in hospital. In my opinion, Mr Hackett, you should be sacked!'

'Your privilege to hold that opinion if you want to – Sir,' Hackett said bleakly. Tate shot him an uncomfortable glance. It was too near to insolence. 'I made an error of judgment,' he went on. 'I admit that. But given what we knew, I can't see anyone forming any different conclusion from the one we came to.'

'You're saying that anybody would have made that mistake?'

'Yes, sir.'

'I don't think so . . .'

'Given the calibre of men we were dealing with, soon as we knew there was bullion coming in . . .'

'You let yourselves get blinkered by it!'

There was a brief pause. 'I suppose so,' Hackett said unhappily.

'I'm telling you so! Call yourself a detective, Mr Hackett? I'd have you booted behind a desk making out Crime Reports!' He paused to let the sting of that work for a while. 'You're luckier than you deserve – that that shipping agent isn't dead!' Hackett nodded wearily. 'Or the policeman!'

'What he did,' Hackett returned almost cruelly, 'was foolish and irresponsible. And he ought to be told as much.'

'Not by you!'

'By me,' Tate rejoined. 'Down to me.'

There was another uncomfortable pause, then the ACC said, 'Essential point you seem to be missing, Mr Hackett – it's not just your getting it wrong we mind. Everybody makes mistakes. But the way you planned it . . . No contingencies! No cover for outsiders!'

'Not enough troops,' Hackett said. He knew that he was lying by omission. The truth was, the bank-roll Latimer had been carrying had never impinged on his mind in any way.

'Balls!' the ACC exploded.

'Thing I always think,' Tate said mildly, 'only person entitled to criticise the bullfighter . . . is the bull!'

The ACC looked at Tate sharply, resenting that, resenting having his ground taken away from him. He looked back to Hackett. 'Even so,' he said, 'you go softly, y'hear? Because I promise you – ramifications of this caper aren't over by a long chalk.'

Hackett said, 'Yes, sir,' wearily. He waited a moment.

'Word with you in private, Mr Tate,' the ACC said.

'Good day, sir,' Hackett said, and left them.

After the door had closed behind him, the ACC said, 'That man . . . needs watching!'

'Think I don't know it?' Tate responded. 'Drives himself, you see. Along a stony road to hell-fire. Can't stop himself. An' when he gets to where he's going he'll be a bloody ugly sight to you an' me. But just at the moment ... he's the best damn Head of Operations I've had!'

'Just as long as you know when to hobble him,' the ACC said.

'Yes, well, that's my job ... isn't it?' They held each other's eyes for a moment. Then the ACC shrugged, and declared his innings.

Hackett was waiting by the cars as Tate came out of the building. He watched his boss come almost wearily down the path, and saw that he was glowering at him; but it was an expression Hackett knew of old, and knew that he was safe.

'Thank you,' sir,' he said quietly.

'You owe me ... and you owe me, Steve,' Tate said in a tired voice.

Hackett nodded. 'How do you want paying?'

'God knows! How about behaving so I don't have to worry about you all the time?'

'Not the way we catch villains – that, sir, is it?'

'Bastard,' Tate growled, and Hackett smiled thinly. 'All right, you make me an offer.'

'Harry Smith,' Hackett said.

Tate paused in the act of opening his car door. 'Steve! ...' he warned.

'I'm still going to have him,' Hackett continued. 'Forty thousand: half a million – what's the odds? It was still his caper.'

'We've had this out before! ...'

'Only now you know I was right,' Hackett rode over him, ' 'cos we brought photographs back to prove it!'

For a moment Tate hesitated, almost bewildered by Hackett's stubbornness. How the hell did you deal with it? He gave up. He climbed into his car and slammed the door. Through the window as he started the engine he heard Hackett's muffled voice calling, 'I'd like your blessing to run Harry as a target, sir.' Tate wound down his window.

'You know where he is?'

'Here or in France.'

'You don't know!'

'I'll find out.'

'You don't even know whereabouts in France he's living!'

'Paris,' Hackett said. 'Vatan got his address for me.'

'So how, in bloody-hell's name how . . . are you going to get him out, Steve? Eh? Tell me how!' Tate waited, but when Hackett didn't answer – couldn't answer – he shook his head in weary impatience, let in the clutch and pulled away.

Watching the car go, Hackett thought, 'God only knows . . . but somehow!' And it wasn't just the old obsession any longer. It was revenge for two men dead and two more in hospital: and for the loss of his own professional pride.

10

Jouffrett was ushered in by the largest PC the station had to offer; silent, blank-faced, but big enough to break the Frenchman's back. The Station Superintendent was taking no chances.

Sitting at the desk in the middle of the barren interview room, Hackett had the gratification of seeing a flicker of recognition and shock on Jouffret's face as he approached. But a flicker was all it was. The Frenchman had himself well under control. He sat on the hard chair in front of the desk and stared with impassive contempt at Hackett, who nodded to the PC indicating that he should wait outside.

'Good afternoon,' Hackett opened pleasantly. Jouffret didn't bother to respond. Hackett smiled. 'Miss Colbert – Louise – asked me to remember her to you.' It was a stab he couldn't resist.

'Bitch,' was all Jouffret said.

And that was all he said for some time. Through all Hackett's solicitude that he should understand British procedures and his right – to phone a solicitor or to remain silent, that he was aware of what the caution he'd been given meant, that anything he did say would be taken down and might be given in evidence . . . through all of it he sat in insolent silence. Even when Hackett began to list the charges which would eventually be brought against him: robbery, assault with intent to commit robbery, unlawful possession of a firearm, the barrels of which had been unlawfully shortened, GBH, resisting arrest, attempted murder of a policeman, and the murder of Peter Robert Newby . . . still he maintained his silence. At the end Hackett paused to let it all sink in, and eventually Jouffret did react.

'Go to 'ell!' he said.

'While you go to prison for life, M'sieur,' Hackett replied evenly. 'Because there's no way that little lot isn't going to send you down for life!' He leaned back from the desk as though it had been a weight he was relieved to be rid of. Jouffret's silence was like a sneer. Hackett was aware of a dangerous temptation to hit the bastard. Slowly he made himself relax. 'So,' he said, 'that's just about everything there is to say about you, M'sieur. Unless you want to tell me anything: make a statement.' He paused, giving Jouffret the chance. The

Frenchman's expression didn't change. 'Fine,' Hackett said. 'So let's talk about Harry.'

Again, he was gratified by a brief flicker in Jouffret's eyes. He reached down to his briefcase and pulled out a large manila envelope. It contained blow-ups of surveillance photographs. He drew one out and placed it on the desk in front of Jouffret. It showed two men sitting together at a table in the dining-room of the Hôtel Boule d'Or: Jouffret himself, and the other whom Hackett's finger lightly tapped. 'Harry,' he said. 'Harry Smith, alias Harold Sloan.'

Jouffret looked at the photo, then back at Hackett and said nothing. Hackett steeled himself, already hating him. There is nothing with which it's more difficult to contend than obstructive silence. It gallops one's patience towards breaking point. It exasperates and infuriates, and makes weary. It mocks all one's efforts; it insults. It induces a feeling of helplessness and impotency which, in another country – perhaps even in his own – would have resulted in Jouffret ending up on the floor having the silence kicked out of him. But close as he came to it, Hackett would not do anything . . . that might give Jouffret's defence lawyer even the tiniest scrap of ammunition. So he cajoled, taunted, threatened, was pleasant and violent by turns, but physically never once even touched the Frenchman.

Jouffret's silence remained obdurate throughout.

In the end Hackett had to give up, simply too drained to continue. He could see Harry slipping away from him, like a fish taking all his line off the spool before he could find the ratchet to stop it. Wearily he regarded the Frenchman and could almost feel the vicious sense of victory emanating from him. There was such undistilled malice there Hackett doubted whether, even if they'd put Jouffret on the floor and that giant of a PC had kicked him half to death, they'd have got anything out of him.

Jouffret was going back to the cells, to magistrates' court in the morning to be remanded, up before a judge and twelve good men and true in a month or two's time, and from there to the top-security wing of Parkhurst, all in silence. Hackett knew it like despair. Maintaining silence was the only victory Jouffret could have over them now. He wasn't doing it to protect Harry. Why should he? Whatever the man's concept of honour, Hackett was bloody sure it didn't embrace that kind of loyalty to Harry. By rights, Hackett thought, he ought to be hating Harry; just as Willie should have hated him, and the rest – the ones who took the risks while Harry took none. And for what? A part-share of forty thousand? . . . It was laughable.

Something flashed in Hackett's mind . . . something someone had said . . . Vatan! 'It 'as to be damn big for 'im to bother, you know?' . . . He could hear the big, friendly Frenchman saying it as they'd sat in the café together '. . . 'as to be damn big for 'im to bother . . .' Damn big, Hackett thought. Forty thousand? Still regarding Jouffret, he wondered: did he know how comparatively little they'd been after?

He said quietly, 'Do you not find it galling, M'sieur, that such an illustrious career as yours should come to an end over such a trivial amount?'

Jouffret said nothing.

'Do you know how much was in the cash bag?' Hackett persisted quietly.

Jouffret looked contemptuously away.

'Forty thousand pounds,' Hackett said. 'Forty thousand pounds.' He made it sound like small change. 'How much was your share going to be, M'sieur? Ten thousand? Less? Hardly enough, I'd have thought, for you to bother. Flying all the way over here for less than ten thousand pounds?'

'You're lyin',' Jouffret said.

They were the first words he'd uttered in over an hour. It was like hearing a stranger's voice. Hackett refused to let the relief or excitement intrude. He shook his head quite calmly.

'You're lyin',' Jouffret said again. But in his eyes, now, Hackett could see the confusion, the doubt . . .

He said, 'No, M'sieur. I'm telling you the truth. You are going to spend the rest of your life in prison – for trying to steal forty thousand pounds.'

'No . . .' Jouffret said. 'What 'Arry tells me . . .' and he paused.

All Hackett's hopes depended on Jouffret talking about Harry. The moment was critical. 'Then Harry conned you, M'sieur,' he said gently.

'Bastard,' Jouffret said.

And Hackett knew that he was home. 'Why? What did he tell you?'

'Big job, 'e said! Damn big job! Bastard!'

Hackett let it eat at him for a moment, then he said gently, 'That's just like Harry. Where'd you meet him?'

'In a bar. In the Boulevard Raspail.'

'When I knew him – he never drank.'

'What 'e was drinkin' was – brown ale . . . in a pub anglais, in the Boulevard Raspail! 'Omesick. 'E don' like Paris, but 'e don' 'ave no money to move. An' 'e don' wan' to go stealin' in France or 'e'll be worse-off than 'ere. So he tells me this big job – bastard!'

'Homesick?' Hackett repeated quietly.

'Eatin' at 'im,' Jouffret said, the memory giving him pleasure now. 'Inside.'

'No money?' Hackett said.

'Not so much no more. Make 'im feel like 'e is nobody. So 'e talk about 'is damn big jobs – make 'im feel big 'imself. Talk!'

'He was big,' Hackett said.

'Not now!'

Hackett wondered how much of it was just bile. This picture of Harry didn't square with the one Hackett carried in his brain; but then, sending Jouffret to knock over forty thousand didn't square with it either. The jigsaw – so complete four days ago – was being disrupted. Somehow, Harry was going out of focus.

'Where is he?' Hackett said. 'In France? Or here?'

'Paris,' Jouffret replied. ''Ow could 'e be 'ere?'

'And this job, why this particular job?'

Jouffret didn't reply. His own bitterness was becoming more important than Hackett's questions. In thinking of Harry he'd suddenly caught an intimation of his own future: caged, with foreigners, pig-ignorant Englishmen like Willie Bellis; surrounded by them . . . until he was an old man. He'd rather have faced the guillotine.

An idea was beginning to move in Hackett's mind, but he could feel Jouffret drifting back towards silence. 'Willie Bellis,' he said urgently. 'Does Harry know about Willie?'

'Who?' Jouffret returned contemptuously.

Hackett pulled another photo out of the envelope. It showed Willie talking to Newby and Jouffret in the hotel bar. He slapped it down in front of the Frenchman. 'Him! Does Harry know that he's dead?'

Jouffret looked at the photo as though it meant nothing to him: not the subject; not the fact of its having been taken. He looked slowly back up to Hackett. 'You can go to 'ell,' he said. 'All you English bastards, go to 'ell!'

And Hackett slowly lent back, knowing that he'd lost him: he'd gone out of reach again.

As Hackett drove back to the office he turned over and over what Jouffret had said. Harry was short of money; felt it necessary to boast of his big jobs; was homesick for England, even to the extent he'd drink brown ale in a phoney English pub on some Parisian boulevard, just to have an illusion of being home again. It all had the ring of pathos to it, which worried him. Whatever Harry had ever been, 'pathetic' was one word he'd never have associated with him. So: if Jouffret's picture was a true one . . . what the hell had the last six years done to Harry? Guessing games!

'What have they done to *me*?' Hackett thought, but immediately decided it was a useless comparison because, psychologically, he and Harry were different animals. But were they? 'Eating inside him,' Jouffret had said, or something like that. In the same way Hackett's obsession had been eating at him? How similar were they? Six years older; six years of losing whichever war they were in . . . 'No,' Hackett thought, 'I'm not pathetic!' The way he drove, gripped the wheel and changed gear had all the violence of a desperate man.

He parked in the car pool and went striding across the tarmac towards the concrete and glass office block. He could see lights on in the Squad room. It made him realise how dull the afternoon had become, and how close to rain all the days seemed to lie now. It depressed him.

Going up in the lift he made his decision. Harry's shortage of money was the key. The gamble was whether or not Harry knew that Willie was dead; and since Jouffret wasn't going to tell him, it was a gamble he had no choice but to take. He recognised that while hope still urged that Harry didn't know, because Jouffret had deemed it prudent not to tell him, his reason argued the other way. Why shouldn't Jouffret have told him? If Harry was the way Jouffret described . . . what danger in telling him? But if Harry had known that Willie was dead, the optimistic side of him countered, he'd have called the job off. Any slight irregularity was like a warning to Harry; and Willie's death might just be called 'a slight irregularity'.

The contradictions and opposing possibilities tore at Hackett's brain. They were unresolvable. So either he gambled and risked losing, or lost anyway. If he'd had time, maybe he'd have been able to think of a better plan, but tomorrow morning Harry was going to pick up the overseas edition of a British newspaper, and read a paragraph about a wages-snatch in the docks that went wrong. And if Hackett didn't move now, that would be when he'd lose him.

Coming into the Main Office he saw Louise. She was dismantling the operation progress board, taking down photos of Jouffret and Newby, and the one of Willie's dead body. She looked up and gave him a brief, casual smile. Since their return from France they'd not been alone at all: hadn't even caught all that many glimpses of each other.

Hackett nodded to her and kept on going towards his office. 'I went to see Bonney,' she called.

He paused. 'How was he?'

'Pretty miserable.'

'Maybe it'll teach him a lesson,' Hackett said callously, and went on into his room. She noticed he didn't shut the door. There was a kind of bleak, hunted quality in him now, she thought; or haunted. It made her feel sorry for him. Flying back together on Wednesday night he'd been more nervously excited than she'd ever remembered seeing him, almost high with their success. Perhaps they should have been warned. Things never went that well. All the same, it seemed unfair. She finished dismantling the board, dropping the photos and bits and pieces into a box file to sort out later, then wandered across to his door. He was at his desk, writing, hunched and engrossed.

She said, 'Does it mean trouble for you?'

He looked up with a slight start. After a flicker of hesitation, he shrugged. 'Some.' His face was taut and pale with strain and tiredness.

'I'm sorry.'

'Not your fault.'

She smiled, and then didn't know whether to stay or go.

'Hey – Louise,' he called. 'Come here and read this.'

She crossed to him and took the sheet of paper he was offering. It was a brief account of the operation, the sort of thing one might read in a newspaper – concise, bald, the bare factual bones . . . until she came to the obligatory police spokesman quote; then, it started to become nonsense. 'A Police Spokesman said that a sixth member of the gang, identified as a man recently released from prison who had been working on the docks, had evaded capture, but that an arrest was expected shortly. He added that until they were able to question the injured victim they wouldn't know whether all the stolen money had, in fact, been recovered.'

She looked up, bewildered. 'Who the hell's this Police Spokesman?'

'Me,' Hackett said. 'How do you like it?'

'Top of the fiction lists – no bother.'

He gave her a strained grin and took the paper back.

'What is that all about?' she asked.

'This is what's going into the Paris edition of tomorrow's *Post*, if they'll play ball.'

'For Harry to read?' she said. Hackett nodded. 'What if he doesn't read the *Post*?'

'He did when he lived here. True-blue is Harry. And the newspaper you read is a lifetime's habit.'

She was still at a loss. 'But what's it supposed to achieve?'

'On its own – nothing. But this, plus something else I've got in mind . . . should, if we're lucky . . .' He paused, momentarily daunted by the amount of luck they needed. 'If we're very lucky . . . tempt Harry to come home.'

Louise was stunned. For a moment she didn't know what to say. It seemed so . . . outlandish; almost naïve. Eventually she asked weakly, 'But what if he already knows Willie's dead?'

'I said – if we're lucky!' Hackett almost snapped back at her. He was sitting, holding his phone about to dial. 'But I've got to try, haven't I?'

She nodded weakly, thinking, 'God, how desperate can he get?'

'If you've got a better idea . . .' he said.

She shook her head, not wanting to get any further involved.

'Right then,' he said. 'Don't lose anything by trying it, do we?' He started to dial a London number. Louise decided she wasn't in the mood to be used as a whipping post, and turned for the door. 'By the way,' he called after her, 'if you've nothing on in half an hour, there's a job you could help me with.'

'It's Sunday,' she said coldly.

'Shouldn't have come in, should you?' he returned, just as cold. She went out, shutting the door loudly behind her. 'Bloody woman!' Hackett thought, and carried on dialling.

He was lucky to catch Norman Culver, the *Post*'s Crime Correspondent, actually at the office. He and Culver had spoken on the phone once or twice before. As soon as Culver came on the line he said, 'About that job in the docks? I've just done a paragraph on it.'

'I wondered if you'd consider incorporating something

for me?' Hackett said, and read Culver the paragraph he'd written.

'You're using me,' Culver accused. 'Planting something.'

'Yes,' Hackett admitted. 'But I only want it in the Paris edition.'

'Still means it'll appear in at least one edition over here.'

'Can you do it?'

'Those last two sentences – they're what's important to you, right?'

'Do they stick out that badly?'

Culver laughed. 'Just tell me no one's going to chew my balls off if we carry them.'

'They're a distortion of the truth,' Hackett said carefully. 'But there are no . . . total lies.' That was only just true: Willie had been a member of the gang, and had evaded capture – in a fairly final sort of way. It wasn't, of course, his arrest that was expected, rather Harry's that Hackett hoped for. As for the money – well, that was hokum.

'All right,' Culver said dubiously. 'Give it me again.'

'I won't forget I'm in your debt,' Hackett said.

'I'll not forget to collect, either,' Culver promised, and took the piece down as Hackett dictated it over the phone.

To fill in time while she waited in the Main Office, Louise started to sort through her intelligence files, discarding the dead wood, bringing others up to date. Hackett had annoyed her and it was best she kept herself busy.

Hackett came quietly out of his office and stood watching her for a moment, without her realising that he was there. She was a hell of an attractive lady, he thought. He felt vaguely ashamed, of making her suffer for something she was in no way responsible for: the devil in himself. It possessed him more frequently than it used to, making him do and say things he always, ultimately regretted. It was as though the degree of control he had over his moods was gradually diminishing, being eroded, and it frightened him a little: made him wonder what was happening to him.

He called softly, 'Louise – I'm sorry.'

She glanced round. He looked so shot-to-pieces with nervous fatigue she was almost appalled. 'My God,' she thought. 'How much longer . . . before he's a burnt-out case?' She said, 'My fault.'

He smiled gratefully and shook his head. 'My nerves. See. I've got to get him, haven't I, Louise?'

'If that's the only answer.'

He nodded slowly. 'Feel like coming?'

'Where to?'

'Evie Bellis.' He grinned at her expression of surprise. 'She's going to write a letter for us.'

Evie was drunk; not rolling or roaring drunk, but unsteady and unco-ordinated, slurring her words slightly. The back room was much as it had been on the previous occasion Louise had called: curtains shut, television on with the sound turned down, radio playing pop music. If anything there seemed to be more junk, a greater degree of untidiness. Coming into the room they felt a sense of claustrophobia. The stale air hung heavy with neurosis, almost tangible: planes of hysterical paranoia lying like smoke in still sunlight. The feeling of time having stopped made Louise uneasy. She felt that prolonged exposure to this atmosphere would start to threaten her own equilibrium.

Evie had laughed when she'd opened the door to them, then she'd stood aside and gestured them in with all the grace of a harridan, still laughing. She followed them into the room and made for the safety of the divan.

'Now we c'n 'ave a party,' she said.

Hackett sat in an armchair across the coffee table from her, and switched off the radio. Louise perched on a dining chair, in the background, out of their way. Hackett had explained what he was hoping to achieve as they'd driven here, and Louise had been honest with him: had said she didn't believe Evie would co-operate, and even if Hackett managed to persuade her, she didn't believe Harry would be taken in. Hackett had shrugged; said it was the best he could do in the time and repeated that nothing was lost by trying. After that they'd not said much for the rest of the journey.

'How are you, Evie?' Hackett asked.

'Me, Flower?' She laughed. 'Couldn' be better.'

He nodded. 'Glad to hear it.'

'Glad to 'ear it,' she echoed, and laughed again. 'You wasn't ever glad to 'ear anythin' 'bout me, Flower. So wha' you bloody wan'? You an' 'er!'

'Got some news for you.'

'Tha's wha' she said last time, an' I don't wanna' 'ear it.'

'We've found Harry.'

She was pouring whisky into her glass. The bottle lurched slightly, slopping on to the table. 'There see wha' you gone an' made me done!'

Hackett took out his handkerchief and calmly leant forward to mop up the spill. 'Thought you'd be glad to hear it,' he said, sounding nothing if not friendly.

She didn't reply. She watched him folding the handkerchief, the wet area on the inside. 'Didn' mind it bein' on the table,' she said eventually. 'Juss don't like losin' it, do I?'

'Too expensive,' Hackett agreed amiably.

'You could've brought a bottle,' she said. 'Not fair, comin' to a party without a bottle.'

'Maybe afterwards,' he said.

'After wha', my Flower?' She was curious but wary. She was less drunk than the outwards signs seemed to suggest. The sagging face wore an expression of amused contempt. In the dull light Louise thought they looked like witch and warlock in a contest of spells.

Hackett didn't answer Evie's question. Too soon for that. Instead he said casually, 'He's still in France. Living in Paris.'

Her reaction was undecided. Eventually she said, 'I tole you so.'

Hackett smiled. 'I've brought his address. I thought you might like to get in touch with him.'

There was a longer pause as her emotions started to become confused. Hackett was up to something, she could tell. All this talk of Harry . . . it was upsetting her. 'Why should I?' she said. ' 'E knows where I am.'

'Oh,' Hackett said innocently. 'Somehow or other I'd got the impression you'd not heard from him. Lost touch.'

She didn't reply. She poured more whisky and began to nibble the edge of her glass as she took one small swallow after another, her eyes starting to brim with self-pity.

'Wasn't that what you told us?' Hackett continued, as though trying to remember. He turned to Louise. 'Isn't that what she told us?'

'I think it was,' Louise said quietly.

'Funny he's not written,' Hackett resumed, looking back to Evie; and then, with a touch of calculated incredulity, 'Not once in four years?'

Evie blinked rapidly, trying to fight back a tear. 'I don' wana talk about 'im. Not much of a bloody party, isn't this!'

'I bet you went to a lot of parties with Harry,' Hackett continued. It was becoming remorseless.

'Yes I did!' she said defiantly.

'Not so many since he's been gone, though? Life's been a bit quieter, I expect. Still, can't go on dancing the light fantastic for ever – any of us.'

'I'm not old!' she flashed back at him.

'No, you just look it,' he returned, without any alteration in his tone.

It came so out of the blue it made Louise catch her breath. Evie's expression was momentarily non-plussed; then, as Louise watched, it slid into pure hate. 'Bugger arf, Mister Hackett!'

'Maybe that's why he left you,' he continued, unperturbed.

' 'E didn'!'

'It wasn't just me he was running away from, Evie! It was you as well!'

' 'E wanned me to go with 'im!'

'Not *one* letter in four years?'

'Juss leave me alone!' Evie shouted.

Hackett smiled and shook his head. 'Not till I've told you why I've come.'

'I don' wanna 'ear anythin' from you – ever.'

'I'm trying to give you a chance to get even with him.'

There was a flicker of hesitation before she said, 'Go to 'ell!'

'All you have to do is write a letter.'

The hesitation was there again. Louise could see the resentful curiosity in Evie's eyes. 'Sayin' what?'

'Well, it won't make much sense to you,' Hackett said casually, 'but the general drift is that Willie's hurt; can't move; but you know where he is; and that somewhere or other he's hidden the money.'

There was a long pause as Evie struggled to take it in.

The silence was such that Louise could hear the faint, faint drone of voices coming from the television: then, from outside, seemingly from a long way away and carried by the wind, the sound of a car starting. There was a chink of glass. She looked sharply back to the divan, and saw Hackett pouring Evie more whisky.

'Willie's dead,' Evie said flatly.

'Harry doesn't know that,' Hackett replied.

'What money?'

'That doesn't matter,' he said. 'Harry'll know.'

There was another, briefer pause. 'You wann 'im to come 'ome,' she said, and Hackett slowly nodded. 'So's you c'n lift 'im?' He nodded again. 'An' you think I'm gonna 'elp?'

'Why not?'

'Sod arf!'

'Why should you protect him, Evie? What do you owe him? After the way he treated you!'

'We 'ad two good year . . .' her voice was on the verge of breaking up.

'Willie would've given you more.'

'Willie!' she said contemptuously.

'He was proud of you, Evie. Pleased as punch to have you. Poor sod! Cared for you. Could've been company for you now. Only he's dead, isn't he? And this is where the joke gets really funny: he's dead because he went back to work for Harry.'

'Workin' for 'Arry? . . .' There was disbelief in Evie's voice.

Hackett nodded. 'You see, Harry may not have kept in touch with you, but he did with Willie: wrote him letters in the nick. And when Willie came out it was all going to be like it was before. Only Harry had this maniac working for him; and one night, just for a bit of a giggle, they pushed Willie in the dock and murdered him, this maniac and another fella. Straight up, Evie, that's the way it was.'

Watching Evie, Louise could see the emotional conflict at work in her. Her face was moving all the time, like soft plastic being moulded and remoulded, creasing and crumpling; while tears welled at her eyes.

'So Harry left you,' Hackett said. 'Then poor old Willie gets the chop. And what are you left with?' He raised the whisky bottle towards her. 'This? All you've got left? You know I saw Harry last week. He didn't look a day different. Why've you not got any mirrors in here, Evie? I wonder how long your liver's going to last out against the booze. Could be years. You're going to have a lonely old age, love. From here on in . . . it only gets worse.'

'Bastard,' she said, in a broken whisper.

'Write the letter.'

'You . . . juss wanna use me!'

'Same way you used me,' Hackett said bleakly. He looked to Louise and nodded to the sideboard. 'Must be some writing paper somewhere.'

Louise delved through the junk in the sideboard drawers, all the clutter of a futile life; nothing to measure forty-odd years by. She felt swamped with depression. In one of the cupboards she found a writing pad of vile, blue paper with envelopes to match, grubby with age. She took it across to Hackett. Evie was quietly blubbering into her drink. Hackett put the pad down on the table in front of her, and laid his ballpoint on top of it. Then he leant across and took the glass out of Evie's hand. She reacted as though she was naked without it, looking for shelter. Hackett picked up the pen and tried to get her to hold it. She shook her head vehemently.

'Shalln't!' she said.

'We don't go until you do.'

'We c'n 'ave a party,' she said again, with a stupid laugh.

Hackett picked up the whisky bottle. 'In five minutes, if you're not writing, this goes down the drain.'

'Bastard!'

Hackett nodded. 'You got what you wanted out of me six years ago. Now I'm going to have what I want out of you. Then we'll call it quits.'

Evie focussed on him with bleary, watery eyes. 'Make you feel good, do it? Bein' as stinkin' rotten as me?'

The self-awareness faintly surprised Louise. She looked to Hackett to catch his reaction, and she could see all the tiredness and self-contempt and bitterness burning out of his face, like heat from a sick man.

'Write the letter, Evie love,' he said. ''Cos when it comes to being stinking and rotten . . . and really nasty – you're not in my league!'

The letter lay between Evie and her next sip of whisky. That was nearly a more powerful incentive than the malice she felt towards Harry. She took the pen in shaky fingers and scrawled her address, then 'Dear Harry . . .' She looked across at Hackett. He nodded, too empty to be pleased, and began dictating.

As they drove away from that grey, abandoned estate for what Louise dearly hoped would be the last time ever, she said dully, 'I think . . . that just living, for a lot of people, must be crueller than any of the tortures the Inquisition ever conceived.'

'Sorry for her?' Hackett said.

'Yes,' she said.

He nodded. 'So would I be . . . if I could afford it.'

She looked at him a moment, impassive but troubled. Then she said quietly, 'What Harry's costing you . . . I hope he's worth it.'

Hackett phoned Vatan the next day. He sidestepped the Frenchman's eagerness for news of the operation, merely confirming that Jouffret, along with others, was now in police custody. Vatan sounded as delighted as a man who'd invested a personal stake in the caper. Hackett found his congratulations faintly embarrassing.

When eventually he got the opportunity, he said, 'I'm afraid I have to ask you another favour, M'sieur . . .' He felt guilty at loading yet something else on to Vatan, who'd already done more than their unofficial co-operation would normally allow, but he was convinced that this was the last favour he would need to ask. It was possible, he explained, that in the next few days Harry Smith alias Harold Sloan might book himself on to a flight to England. If that happened, he asked, was there any way someone in the Paris Judiciaire could learn of it, and alert either Vatan or himself?

Vatan gave the impression that it wouldn't be difficult at all. He had friends in the Paris force. It could be done quietly and with no kick-back by using the Old Boy net. Hackett was careful not to embarrass Vatan by asking how it would be done. That was something it was best he remained ignorant about, besides not being any of his business. But he did know, as a matter of historical interest, that after the war the French police had inherited from the Gestapo a vast network of phone taps, which even included taps on public call-boxes, which they'd retained and still, from time to time, found a use for.

The days which followed created in him the same edgy restlessness as that which he experienced before an operation. In terms of work there was only the clearing up. Croft, Stott and the younger man, who turned out to be Stott's brother-in-law, all made detailed statements. Jouffret maintained his silence. There were reports to be read, signed and passed on up to Tate. The writing of

Hackett's own report took most of Tuesday. It was one of the most considered documents he was ever likely to produce. That afternoon the body of a man was discovered in suspicious circumstances at a farm to the north of the City, and suddenly there was another, small operation getting under way. Hackett delegated the handling of it to one of his Chief Inspectors, while he stayed by the phone and waited.

If Vatan hadn't come back to him by the end of the week, he'd decided, he'd call it a day and live with the disappointment the best he could. But until then . . . sometimes he marvelled at how strong the capacity to hope remained in him, despite everything. It was a bloody good job, he thought, because there were times enough, like now, when hope was all he had.

Vatan phoned late on Wednesday afternoon. He was in a state of contained excitement. Hackett knew the news was good as soon as he heard his voice.

'You are in luck, M'sieur. 'Arold Sloan 'as booked 'imself a seat on a British Airways flight, Paris–'Eathrow, departin' Paris at eleven 'undred 'ours tomorrow.'

Hackett's brain kept bouncing the words back into his ears. This had to be the way you felt when they told you you'd won the Treble Chance, he thought. Harry was coming home.

'You're sure? . . .'

'Quite sure, M'sieur. Positive.'

'Christ Almighty,' Hackett said.

Vatan laughed. 'You 'aven't got long, so we 'ave to work fast – eh?' Hackett loved the man for that 'we'. 'I 'ave a contact, an Inspecteur, in Paris who could be available, if you are goin' to send someone . . .'

'Too right I'm going to send someone,' Hackett said. 'I want him to be watched right on to that plane!'

Vatan said drily, 'I think, mebbe, I will be jealous of

the Inspecteur – eh? Am I right?'

'She'll be leaving tonight,' Hackett said, and Vatan laughed again.

In the Main Office folk froze in what they were doing as Hackett's voice yelled out of his open door, 'Louise!'

Startled, she began to rise, embarrassed to be the sudden centre of attention. Hackett appeared at his door.

'How fast can you pack that little bag of yours?' he said. 'I want you and . . .' his gaze briefly searched the room, 'Dukes . . . in Paris – by this evening.'

11

Paris was bright and crisp in the thin, autumn sunlight. It was going to be a day, Louise thought, when one should be walking the boulevards, not stuck in a car; or perhaps be playing boules or admiring Rodin, or drinking coffee at a pavement table for what might be the last time of the year, but not to be in the Rue Lorette, watching the entrance to a dreary building fifty yards down the street.

23 Rue Lorette was where Harry Smith rented a small apartment on the second floor, facing the street. Its three grimy windows sported dark green shutters, open, that looked as though they'd disintegrate if anyone tried to move them. On the inside of the glass was net. There were flower boxes on the window sills, but no sign of any flowers. The neighbourhood had never been fashionable. The street was narrow, the tall buildings cutting out most of the sun. The apartment houses were featureless and grey with a century's city-smoke encrusted into the fabric of the stone.

The street itself was quiet. But it lay just off a broad avenue that was already choked with traffic, visible from where they sat, parked three-quarters on the pavement in a line of cars belonging to residents. They were in a Peugeot. Louise sat in the passenger seat, Dukes at the back, and behind the wheel was Inspecteur Paul Blain, the contact arranged by Vatan, who'd met them at Roissy the previous evening.

Blain was in his thirties, brusque and dry, a chain smoker. He had the air of a man who was prepared to tolerate their presence because he'd been told to, but found it all slightly irregular and an imposition. Louise had tried to explain who and what Harry was, and Blain had shrugged as though he wasn't much interested. Then he'd said, 'If 'e'es such a big robber, why's 'e livin' in a place like this?' And he gestured to the drab buildings all around them. It was a question Louise hadn't been able to answer, and conversation had lapsed again.

To give himself time to check in Harry needed to be at the airport by ten forty-five. In order to make that comfortably, he'd have to leave by nine forty. Louise glanced at her watch and saw that that gave him another forty minutes. Their job, once he started to move, was to stay with him all the way, then having watched him on to the plane and the plane take off, to phone their operational base at the Crime Squad Office who would pass the message on to Hackett at Heathrow that Harry was on his way.

Louise stifled an urge to yawn, and reflected that after a while lack of sleep was something the body grudgingly became used to. A clanking, grinding street-cleaning vehicle turned in from the avenue and began to crawl towards them on the other side of the road, with its brushes whirling along the gutter, and hoses spurting water. Its bulk obscured another vehicle which had turned in behind it, and it wasn't until the cleaning truck had passed number 23 that they saw there was a taxi drawing up outside the building. The driver got out, crossed to the doorway, and pressed one of the bell buttons.

They watched in silence. There was an uncertain air of tension. If that cab was for Harry, Louise thought, it was much too early. The driver had got back inside again and was waiting. On the other side of the street the cleaning truck ground past them like a great, mechanical sloth eating garbage. Its roar was deafening. Suddenly, out of number 23, a figure emerged: a man; wearing a raincoat and trilby, and carrying a small, battered overnight case. Her surprise registered on Louise's face. It was Harry; she was sure that was Harry! Blain glanced at her. The cleaning truck was still swamping them with its roar. Louise looked back at him and nodded.

They watched the cab execute a tight, three-point turn, then head off back towards the avenue. Blain started the car and they gently began to follow.

'Giving himself plenty of time,' Dukes said, and Louise nodded. It really was almost absurdly early.

They left Paris through a grim sprawl of decaying outer suburbs and joined the autoroute north at the Porte de la Chapelle. From there it was less than twenty minutes to the airport, a fast, straight run-in. The taxi had made no detours, hadn't stopped anywhere, so from the look of it Harry was going to be at the airport with nearly an hour to spare. Louise knew of people who were like that, who had to be at the station or wherever with bags of time in hand, but she was surprised to find Harry was one of them.

They stayed nearly half a mile behind the taxi all the way, and were confident that Harry hadn't clocked them. By shortly after ten Blain was dropping them outside the airport check-in doors, before taking the Peugeot up ramps to the car park stack on top of the impressive terminal. Entering the lower Departure Level Louise and Dukes eventually spotted Harry and saw that he'd finished checking in and was strolling past the Air France desks towards the extraordinary moving footway which carried one through a glazed tube in the centre of the circular concourse up to the customs and passport check on the next level.

'Not hanging about, is he?' Louise said.

They waited until he was absorbed among passengers on the travelator, and well ahead, then casually followed. Coming out on to the main Departure Level they were in time to see him in a queue of passengers filtering through the police and passport check towards the lounge and duty-free shops beyond. He'd made for here more quickly than Louise had expected. She felt a sudden, vague snatch of apprehension. They were baulked. Until Blain joined them from parking the car they'd not be able to get through the passport check, and Harry was going to be out of sight in a moment. She looked at her watch. There were still another forty minutes. The plane wouldn't be taking on passengers yet so it was all right; they had plenty of time.

'Bet you he's run out of smokes,' Dukes said. 'Wants to get 'em cheap in the duty-free.'

Louise smiled and nodded. But at the same time her eyes were on the flow of passengers emerging from the travelator, impatient for Blain to appear.

The Special Branch office at Heathrow was a plain, featureless room behind an unmarked door. It contained three desks, two filing cabinets, another metal cabinet sporting a combination lock, three telephones and a notice board bearing one or two posters and photographs of people Special Branch were on the look out for. Through the window, between the open slats of venetian blinds, could be seen the edge of one of the roof observation terraces, already thronged with people: and beyond – the criss-cross web of runways and grass.

Hackett, Ikey Baer and Tom Cubbon glanced incuriously around the office. Its regular inhabitants had done nothing to personalise it. It was an anonymous space, like a waiting room. But it was enough for their needs: a phone to keep them in touch with their operational base back at the Crime Squad office; and somewhere to bring Harry for the formalities to be conducted.

Taggart, the Special Branch officer playing host for the morning, gestured vaguely around. 'Make yourselves at home.' There was a touch of sarcasm in his voice.

Hackett smiled tightly. 'Thanks.' He dumped his briefcase on one of the desks and wandered across to the window. A BA One-Eleven was taxiing towards the terminal, while beyond it a Seven-Four-Seven – belonging to some Arabian airline, judging by its markings – hurled into view and out again on its take-off. Even through the double-glazed windows the roar of the plane's engines vibrated inside the room.

'When's your man due?' Taggart asked.

'Eleven forty-three,' Hackett said. He looked at his watch: over an hour yet: one hour and exactly seventeen minutes, providing there was no delay at Roissy. It was too long, as always; waiting was always too long. Though what was one hour and seventeen minutes after six years and more? He found the prospect of confronting Harry oddly unsettling, as though it was bound to be anticlimactic. He doubted that Harry would make a fuss. It would be quiet and all over – just like that. He'd lived with the desire for this morning for so long now, though, it frightened him – that he might find an emptiness, once the desire had been fulfilled.

He turned away from the window, uncomfortable and restless. 'Going to look over the ground,' he said, and walked out of the office.

Ikey and Cubbon looked at each other and Ikey gave a barely perceptible shrug. He pulled a pack of cards out of his pocket and waved them at Taggart. The SB man grinned and nodded. They pulled up chairs and sat around his desk, playing poker.

Blain escorted Louise and Dukes through the passport control into the Transfer Level beyond. It was like coming into a busy shopping centre. There were shops to buy men's and women's clothes, books, toys, records, gifts, smokes, food and drink, as well as bars and a restaurant. Everywhere was thronging with people: a tight jumble of colour and movement, breaking around rows of seats which faced the huge windows overlooking the airport.

They stood quite still letting their eyes slowly travel over the chaos of the scene. Somewhere, in all of that, was Harry. But it was hopeless. Amidst so much fractured movement, and at this distance, their gaze stood no chance. According to Louise's watch there was still just over half an hour to go. The embarkation gate wouldn't be open yet, so Harry had to be either somewhere in this crush of folk, or maybe sitting in the BA satellite lounge. Something was nagging at the back of Louise's mind, something that wouldn't quite come into focus. She battled with it for a moment, but then realised that she was wasting time.

'We'd better split up,' she said.

She and Dukes took the concourse while Blain went to check the satellite. As Dukes darted from shop to shop, bar to bar, Louise eased her way through the milling passengers: weaving and pivotting, occasionally standing still to let her glance linger over a particular scene; at other times looking quickly one way, then the other, and then another, hoping with each new aspect to surprise her eyes with a sudden recognition of Harry. She didn't. She caught no glimpse of him; and minutes were passing.

It wasn't until her gaze happened to alight on a departures board that the thing still nagging in her mind came clear. As they'd entered the check-in hall Harry had been nowhere near the British Airways desks; he'd been leaving the Air France section. And there, on the board, was Air France Flight 850, Paris–London, departing at ten-forty hours.

'He's changed his ticket,' she thought. 'That's why he came early . . . he's flying Air France . . . takes off twenty minutes sooner, so it'll land twenty minutes sooner . . .' And then the rest of it hit her: Hackett was expecting Harry to arrive around eleven-forty: at around eleven-*twenty* he might not be in position. She looked at her watch. It was just after ten-forty. She crossed quickly to the windows, and there, just starting to taxi away from one of the satellites, she saw a blue and white French Airbus.

The level of near-panic in her subsided slightly, as she realised that she had plenty of time to get the message through to Hackett. If Harry was on that Airbus, nothing had changed. She turned away and went hurriedly to find Dukes and Blain.

Neither of them had seen Harry. In Louise's mind it confirmed her suspicion, but to be as sure as they could be she asked Blain if he'd check with the staff on the boarding gate to see whether they remembered anyone fitting Harry's description. While he was gone she and Dukes tried to fathom what had made Harry do it. He'd not clocked them, they were certain, so the only explanation they could find was that it was simply the habit of a surveillance-conscious man. Blain returned with the news that one of the girls on the gate thought she remembered a man answering Harry's description. That was good enough, Louise decided. Now all she had to do was let Hackett know: ring the Crime Squad office, give them the message to pass on. It was ten fifty-one: half an hour before the Airbus landed.

It took Blain just over four minutes to find an overseas telephone operator who was free to handle the call. Louise gave her the number of Crime Squad office and was directed into one of the reserved kiosks. She picked up the phone and waited. A minute went by; a minute and a half; it was almost two minutes before she heard the girl saying, 'I am sorry but I cannot reach your number.'

'Why?' Louise said faintly.

'All lines out of London are engaged. Per'aps you would care to try again later?'

And that was when Louise's nightmare began.

The Immigration Officer looked down at Hackett's Warrant Card, then back up to Hackett. 'Morning, Superintendent,' he said.

Hackett nodded in return. 'BA Flight 601,' he said.

The Immigration Officer looked at his watch. 'In from Paris, 'bout thirty-five minutes.'

'There'll be someone on it,' Hackett said. 'A man. Who I'm here to lift.'

'Name?'

'Likely . . . Harold Sloan.'

'British?'

'Right down to the soles of his feet.'

'Help yourself.'

'You'll be on, will you?' Hackett said. 'When they come through?'

The Immigration Officer nodded.

'Mind if I stand behind you, Put another of my blokes over there?'

'Wherever suits you best.'

Hackett nodded. 'Thanks.'

At just about that same moment the Air France Airbus was beginning to let down into the Heathrow approach pattern.

'Yes!' Louise said, her teeth gritted in exasperation. 'But please, please, just keep trying!' Her watch told her she now had less than ten minutes. 'Bloody GPO!' She thought. Base and Hackett would be wondering why she'd not called by now. She'd racked her brains to think of some way of contacting Hackett direct . . . but even if she'd rung Heathrow Airport Administration it would have taken too long to get the number of the Special Branch office; they probably wouldn't have given it to her anyway..

Nine minutes.

'God in Heaven,' she thought, 'Harry's going to *make* it!' All thanks to an overloaded telephone line! She couldn't believe the absurdity of the situation. She tried to anticipate Hackett's reaction, but it got so awful her mind shied away from it. Outside the kiosk she was aware of Dukes and Blain impotently waiting, pacing, looking at their watches. 'Even Blain's caught it,' she thought . . .

'Come on!' she said. 'Come *on*!'

'Your number is ringin' now,' the operator said.

Louise felt momentarily as though she might faint. She could actually hear the ringing, that steady, monotonous ringing! . . .

A voice said, 'Regional Crime Squad . . .'

Speaking as calmly and precisely as she could, Louise said, 'This is Detective Sergeant Colbert in Paris, I have an urgent message for Detective Superintendent Hackett at Heathrow Airport. You have just eight minutes to get it to him – say again: eight minutes. Message is . . .'

Hackett and Ikey passed through the door in the flimsy partition which cut off the Customs Hall from the rest of the Terminal One Arrival Area. Hackett knew it was early to be taking up position, and he was concerned that they'd not had any message from Louise yet; but movement gave him purpose in this otherwise too vacuous time.

There was a steady stream of arrivals passing through the hall, one plane load flowing into the next, and more coming on behind. The size of the customs officers' problem could be grasped in an instant.

Struggling in this tide that bore against them they were only half-way down the hall when they heard Cubbon's shout. 'Sir!' Hackett froze. Something in the urgency of Cubbon's voice . . . They turned and saw him flailing towards them, almost mowing people down in his desperation to get through. Gulping for breath as he reached them, he said, 'Just got a message from Louise . . . He's on an Air France flight . . . due to arrive eleven twenty-two . . .'

Hackett looked sharply at his watch. It was after eleven twenty now. His face jerked to the passengers streaming past them. 'He's among this lot!' he exclaimed almost horrified.

'No, sir . . .' Cubbon looked as if he didn't want to say it. 'Air France use Terminal Two.'

There was the briefest of pauses as it sank in. 'Oh Christ . . .' Hackett said.

They hit the pads which electronically activated the

doors with such speed that the doors barely had time to open before they were through, and pounding along the front of the building. A party of Japanese boarding a coach suddenly found themselves shot through with hurling figures. People on the central island waiting for minibuses to take them out to the Long Stay Car parks watched with uneasy, bemused curiosity. Cubbon collided with a luggage trolley, broadside on, and went down amidst an avalanche of cases. Hackett and Ikey kept on running.

Over an access road, past a bicycle shed, along the side of offices, across another road, their insides jarring as each foot hit the ground and a burning in their chests, they came, at last, through an inconspicuous door into Terminal Two. They were at the bottom of concrete steps. Without a pause Hackett went charging upwards. He came into a short, sloping corridor, turned the corner at the end and found himself suddenly entering the Arrival Hall.

It was crowded, made worse by the fact that alterations and re-fitting work was in progress. Large areas were cut off so that people were crammed into narrow through-ways which quickly became snarled in tight, jostling cross-currents around the waiting friends and relatives of arriving passengers.

People were streaming out of the customs hall. Hackett began to shoulder his way through them, looking now at each arrival, trying to focus on the blur of faces as they passed, desperately willing one of them to be Harry. Cases banged his calves and shins; shoulders jarred against him; a voice swore at him in French. He kept going, almost brutally thrusting on, head jerking from side to side, momentarily deceived by the odd, half-glimpsed profile, hope and disappointment spurting hot and cold within him, and his desperation mounting. He emerged into the customs hall and still hadn't spotted him. He scanned the passengers waiting for their baggage, and scanned them again, sweating, shaking and gulping, trying to blink away the patina of exertion that misted his gaze . . . and scanned them a third time to convince himself that Harry really wasn't there.

At the baggage check he saw two customs officers standing momentarily idle. He sprinted across to them, his Warrant Card out and raised as he arrived. 'Air France, just in from Paris!' he said. His urgency made their reaction seem delayed as though they were in slow motion. They glanced at each other, then back to him over his card, still held up to their faces like a challenge.

'Starting to come through now,' one of them said.

Hackett swung back to face the body of the hall. He was still sweating and trembling. There had to be well over a hundred people crowding his field of vision, more pouring in from the immigration control. Somewhere among them, either right now, or at any moment, Harry would be there; somewhere among them Harry *had* to be there! Hackett was suddenly and utterly certain of it, with a surge of relief that came dangerously near to swamping him. 'Made it,' he thought. 'Bloody well made it, Harry!'

The scene before him had no focal point: it seethed. Wherever he looked, movement frayed the edges of his vision. Trying to pick out details like the features of a man's face was a visual battle against the constant jostle and mass of colours. He began to move forward towards the baggage wheels where he could wait without looking conspicuous. Then, ahead of him, he suddenly saw Ikey, standing by one of the chutes down which cases came slithering in a steady stream. Their glances never met, but Hackett knew he'd been read. He carried on, weaving between overloaded baggage trolleys and piles of stacked cases and dense clusters of passengers, while babble tangled with the noise of feet filling the lofty hall.

He was heading for the second baggage wheel, but before he got there . . . for just a moment, between the heads and hats that shuttered across his view – he saw Harry. It pulled him up with an extraordinary sense of shock, like the shock a bridegroom feels at the sudden reality of his bride as she walks down the aisle to join him: the almost disbelieving, 'It *is* her; she *has* come . . .' Only as Hackett thought, 'That's *him*!' it was with the relief of so much hate about to be consummated, and not with love. He stood stock-still, almost dazed, waiting for just one more glimpse to confirm the sighting.

Wearing his raincoat and trilby, carrying his battered overnight case, Harry was making his way steadily and unhurriedly towards the 'Nothing to Declare' Green Channel through customs. He appeared not to have seen Hackett yet. Between them was maybe fifty yards crowded with people and trolleys, which was too far and too full of obstacles for Hackett to make any move. The six-year wait had become a matter of seconds now, but Hackett knew the game was still wide open. He glanced towards Ikey, but couldn't see him for the crush. He wondered where the hell Cubbon was, not to know that the latter's collision with the luggage trolley had put him out of it with a wrenched knee. All Hackett did know was that Harry was maybe ten yards nearer while his own troops were nowhere in sight.

He turned slightly and fixed his gaze on one of the Green Channel regulation boards across the hall. At the very edge of his vision he could still see Harry coming on, though he appeared not to be looking at him at all. He felt a tightening in his stomach, because until he actually put his hand on Harry's shoulder . . . the game was still wide open. Streams of people broke against him and passed on either side. Figures bobbed at the periphery of his vision, momentarily obscuring Harry. Resisting the urge to look directly at him was getting harder. Harry was less than thirty yards away now. 'Go,' Hackett told himself. 'Go – now!' He began to move, casually slanting across towards an intercept point at the entrance to the Green Channel. And it was just about at that moment that Harry saw him.

It took Harry another couple of seconds to convince himself that it actually was Hackett moving in ahead of him. It was over six years since he'd seen him; but Hackett hadn't changed much, and whatever doubt Harry momentarily allowed himself to feel, it had more to do with hope than genuine uncertainty. Involuntarily he checked his step and glanced around very quickly. There was no one else he'd swear to be a policeman, but several who might be. Still walking, he looked back to Hackett, and for one of the few times in his life Harry Smith felt fear. Hackett! Of all the policemen there were in the world – bloody Steve Hackett! What in hell was he doing here? As far as he could tell, Hackett hadn't seen him yet – or had he? This was too much of a bloody coincidence. He realised he'd slowed to a crawl and was sweating. It made him conspicuous. He had to keep going. But what was that bastard copper doing here? . . .

He thought of Willie Bellis, and Evie, and Evie's letter . . . and although he couldn't perceive any direct link to Hackett he realised he was feeling sick. Then he thought of four years rotting in France just to be safe from the likes of Hackett, and he felt sick with anger as well as with fear: if all that was to be for nothing! Four years in that bastard country, growing older and poorer, feeling his alienation eating his guts out – all for nothing? . . . He couldn't allow himself to contemplate it. Hackett still appeared not to have seen him, so he forced himself to believe it might be mere coincidence. He wished he'd never come. But it was too late to turn round, and maybe, if he stayed calm . . . He was Harry Smith, the best, and he'd always beaten Hackett before: all he had to do was stay calm – and unobtrusive . . .

A group of Dutch tourists were overtaking him. He quickened his pace slightly to keep up with them, and gravitated to the side of the group furthest away from Hackett.

They played the game for nearly a minute, neither looking at the other, both pretending to be unaware, while drawing inexorably closer. Harry was reluctant to break and run because if this *was* coincidence, if Hackett *hadn't* seen him, he'd be drawing attention to himself for no reason. But his nerves were starting to scream. As far as Hackett was concerned, the closer he could get to Harry before allowing the confrontation to become overt, the less likelihood there'd be of his losing him. Even now, if Harry decided to take it on his toes, there were too many people and cases and trolleys between them for Hackett to be sure he could reach him before Harry gained the exit. All the same, he knew Harry had seen him and, judging by his behaviour, had no intention of putting his hands up; so a break was bound to come. The only question was how close would Harry let him get before his nerve snapped. As the distance between them steadily decreased Hackett felt the moment growing critical and again, only now with an edge of desperation, he wondered where the hell Ikey and Cubbon were.

Ikey was behind Harry, striding after him and closing fast, and finally it was he who blew the game apart. That instinct which had kept Harry Smith safe all his life suddenly, inexplicably, made him glance backwards. And barging through the straggling possession of passengers he saw a man dressed in a tweedy, leather-patched jacket and slacks, who wasn't pushing a trolley, wasn't carrying a suitcase or even an attache case, and Harry knew him for what he was, again with that instinct that never failed him. Suddenly it stopped being coincidence: he didn't know how it had happened, but the reason Hackett was there was to lift *him*! No realistic alternative existed any more. He looked towards his enemy and judged that he was still over fifteen yards away. A luggage trolley was cutting across his path. For a second Hackett's view was obstructed, and Harry hurled himself towards the exit.

Ikey shouted, 'Sir!'

Hackett dodged round the trolley and saw the sudden burst of movement, the running figure tearing a path through the people in front of him. He yelled, 'Stop him!' and launched himself in pursuit. Harry had at least ten yards on him, and it was too much. Hackett was younger and fitter and had more speed than Harry, but he knew the distance was too great. As he ploughed into the bewildered passengers reeling in Harry's wake, he saw his quarry was already into the narrow neck of the funnel leading out to the main concourse. In mounting, angry desperation he began to shoulder and claw his way after him.

In the narrowest, most congested section of the passageway, Harry deliberately dropped his case. A woman behind him tripped over it. She staggered and grabbed for the nearest support which was a trolley. As she fell she dragged it with her, so that it was slewing sideways across the passage and tilting. A case started to slither from on top. The man in charge of the trolley made a grab to save it, but was buffeted sideways by the crush of folk at his back. As a small-scale example of the domino theory, it was classic. Emerging into the Arrival Hall Harry could hear the escalating chaos behind him, but he didn't look back. He had to get out, get off the airport, and however long that confusion delayed Hackett was all the time he had.

Forcing his way through the crush of waiting people and those others struggling to pass them, he crossed the concourse and went through the electronically operated glass doors that gave into the exit tunnel. He was conscious of having to gulp for breath, while sweat stung his eyes. He wasn't used to this sort of exertion. His legs felt weak, but he couldn't rest yet: not till he was in the back of a taxi and leaving the airport behind. Then he could afford to rest, when he knew for sure that he'd beaten Hackett; and maybe then he'd be able to make sense of what had happened.

Not quite running, but at a fast, lunging pace, he went down the sloping tunnel and came out into the grey, cold day. He was on the concourse that ran along the front of the terminal, where airport buses were filling with people, and crowds thronged the pavement in front of the check-in doors. Beyond the buses, and the passengers milling around the shelters, he saw a line of taxis taking on fares at the rank. He started towards them, then saw the length of their queue, and knew there were too many people for the number of cabs. He might still have kept on going to try to queue-jump, but then suddenly he saw a blue and white police car parked between the bus-lane and the taxis, and that pulled him up short. Coincidence? Or was that copper on the look-out for him? Today, as far as Harry was concerned, nothing was coincidence, not any more.

For an instant he felt a wave of panic surging through him, and out there in the open he seemed suddenly too exposed and vulnerable. He swung back towards the terminal. With no way of knowing how big a net Hackett had spread, at least in the terminal he could lose himself in the crowds. He began to walk, fast, back towards the building. He'd only got half way when, with a sense of shock and near despair, he saw Hackett again, running from the mouth of the exit ramp. He should have continued to walk. He didn't. He hadn't enough control left in him. He began to run . . . and Hackett saw the movement.

Harry went ploughing and crashing through people and luggage, stumbling and staggering on. Several times he nearly went down. Someone he rammed aside turned and hit him. He kept going; and reaching the building plunged in through the glass doors to find himself in the Alitalia check-in. It was a smallish hall, packed with dense queues stretching from the check-in desks, and mountains of cases and bags cluttering the floor. The only way out was beyond the desks, and only then if you were armed with a ticket and boarding card. Harry floundered, his brain whirling in panic like a merry-go-round gathering speed. People were beginning to take note of the rumpus behind him. He looked back once and saw that Hackett had almost reached the doors . . . while he was trapped! He could see freedom across the partition which divided this hall from the next, where an escalator rode upwards, but there was no way through to reach it, and Harry wasn't the vaulting kind. Only with Hackett at his back he was anything he had to be, and he went like a bull smashing a path through the queues, heading for that partition.

It was chest-high. Without breaking step he jumped towards it, got his hands on the top and forced his body up into the air, twisting himself over it. A woman started to scream stupidly. A man's voice was shouting . . . one of Harry's hands lost its hold and he crashed across the partition, falling on to his back on the other side. The impact smashed the wind out of him and he gave a sharp cry of pain. He rolled over on to his stomach and somehow managed to get back on to his feet. Momentarily he was vaguely aware of faces turned towards him, shocked and uncomprehending faces . . . then the escalator came into focus, only feet away. Still winded, he dived for it, as he heard a grunt and the scrambling sound of Hackett coming over the partition behind him.

Harry went charging up the escalator on legs that felt they were about to give out, sobbing with exhaustion. Half way up he brutally dragged a girl backwards off her step, tripped her, and sent her sprawling down into Hackett's path with a scream of terror.

At the top he found himself re-emerging into the crowded Arrival Hall. The fact that this was somewhere he'd been before added to his desperation – the feeling that he was going round in circles and getting nowhere. But it was choked with people, and still he clung to the idea that in a big enough crowd he could lose himself. He turned towards the information desks and the passage leading to the departure gates beyond, and started to labour his way through the crush . . . and that was when the first pain hit him.

It wasn't like the pain of falling on his back. It wasn't like any pain he'd ever known before. It was a spasm in his chest of such pure agony it made him cry out, and for as long as it lasted he couldn't breath. His legs continued to carry him forward, though mentally that first stab seemed to have robbed him of all conscious, locomotory power. It began to fade, as spasms do, only for him to be hit by a second, just as savage, snatching his breath away and holding him in a momentary vice of indescribable pain. He was beginning to move like a drunken man, unable to help himself as his legs started to succumb to the attack. The BA information desks were tilting through his view, which was how he knew he was falling.

He felt his knees hit the ground, and then the pain came for the third time, worse by far than either of the previous spasms. He knew it was his heart; and all he could do was wait for the next attack, and the next, and whichever it was that was going to kill him.

At first people ignored him. They either skirted or stepped over him, with the odd foot giving him an accidental kick; but by the time Hackett got there a ring was beginning to form, faces gawping at the writhing figure. Sweating and heaving for breath, Hackett watched him a moment, not understanding. Then, gradually, he recognised what he was seeing. Harry was twisting and moaning, his fingers dragging at his collar and tie. Hackett hesitated a second longer, wondering whether he was faking it; but the man's face was so grey, contorted in such agony that he knew it had to be the real thing.

He thought, 'Christ – no!'

Then he was on his knees beside him, ripping open Harry's shirt at the neck.

'Somebody get a doctor!' he yelled. 'It's his heart! For God's sake somebody – get an ambulance!'

Whether anyone acted he didn't know. The circle bulged and eddied round them, people staring with ghoulish fascination and curiosity, but holding back, not wanting to become involved. Hackett cradled Harry's head in his arms, alone with him in the middle of fifty or sixty folk. 'Someone get an ambulance!' he yelled again in desperation. Harry recognised the voice and opened his eyes. 'Just hang on,' Hackett said.

'Pain . . .' Harry whispered, and his face suddenly contorted as another spasm gripped him.

'I know,' Hackett said. 'Help's coming. You just hang on.'

'Your fault,' Harry said, 'this.' And he managed a malicious, twisted grin.

'You don't bloody die on me, y'hear?' Hackett returned vehemently. Harry just laughed. Close-to like this, face to face for the first time in over six years, Hackett could see the age in Harry's face: lines where he remembered only blandness, shadows and bags where once there'd been bloom. Beneath the sweat there was an air of physical corruption about him that was faintly disgusting. And then Hackett saw something that hit him like a revelation: the collar of Harry's shirt was frayed. It seemed to answer so many questions, to put so much into some kind of perspective. Harry was broke. Hackett wondered what he'd hocked to pay his air fare, and suddenly he felt such a weight of sadness on him it was like despair.

Not half a million in silver bullion – just forty thousand in notes; not Harry Smith, the man he remembered – only the ghost of him; not even Hackett himself, the man he once was – only a wasted burnt-out shell of him.

He cradled Harry's head as fresh pain made the man writhe and groan. 'Just hang on,' he said desperately, 'we'll make it.' Fifty or sixty folk looked on, hoping to see a death. 'Don't die on me,' Hackett said again. 'We'll make it!'

Through his agony Harry somehow managed to say, 'We?'

Before Hackett could respond there was a commotion in the circle around them: and he was still kneeling, still cradling Harry's head, in the way one might a dying lover's, as the first ambulance man arrived.